# Rebecca's Daughters

# DYLAN THOMAS

# *Rebecca's Daughters*

With
Illustrations
by
FRITZ EICHENBERG

**A New Directions Book**

Manufactured in the United States of America
First published clothbound in 1966 by Little, Brown & Co. Reissued in an illustrated edition by New Directions in 1982.

Published simultaneously in Canada by George J. McLeod, Ltd., Toronto

Library of Congress Cataloging in Publication Data

Thomas, Dylan, 1914–1953.
  Rebecca's daughters.
  (A New Directions Book)

  I. Eichenberg, Fritz, 1901–    II. Title.
PR6039.H52R4   1982    791.43'72    82-7986
ISBN 0-8112-0852-4                 AACR2

New Directions Books are published for James Laughlin
by New Directions Publishing Corporation,
80 Eighth Avenue, New York 10011

# Rebecca's Daughters

*H*eavy rain in a wild wind. And winter dusk. Nothing but the torn and blowing sheets of rain, and the wind ripping and wailing.

Then, through the rain and wind, the clopping of horses' hooves and the rattle of wheels, and a closed chaise dashes past us into the wild dusk. Close, we see it as a great rattling blur in the rain and wind; then it is gone.

Now we see it, through the rain, approaching us down a narrow, pooled and rutted country road, bare trees each side of it, tossing in a temper. Blown broken branches scrabble and scrape the wood-work and windows as the chaise lurches on, the horses streaming and breathing out clouds in the dusky gusty cold. Up spurt the waves of mud.

The chaise rounds a corner of the narrow road. And, from the driver's box, lurching and tilting as we go, we see before us another rough stretch of road in the rain. And, some way ahead, a sign-post where the road divides in two directions.

The figure of a man, hat well pulled down and cloak buttoned high, stands beneath the sign-post, a desolate, dripping figure, his cloak swirling about him.

He steps into the middle of the road and holds up his hand.

We see him from the driver's box, looking down along the wet horses' backs. And we see the driver's mittened, soaking hands pull hard on the reins. The chaise draws up.

Of the two dividing roads before us, one is of fairly even surface, the other little more than a bogged and pitted farm-track.

The sign-post arm which points to the rude rough road, says: PEMBROKE.

The cloaked man moves, slushing through pools, to the side window of the chaise, comes close to it, peers through the blurred and streaming glass.

Seen through the glass, Anthony Raine lowers the window. He is a good-looking young man in the scarlet of an Army officer of the period 1843.

Now, from the interior of the chaise, we look past Anthony out of the lowered window to see the face of the cloaked man, Sir Henry Price-Parry, outside.

Sir Henry makes his gruff voice loud to sound above the wind and rain.

'Good evening, sir . . .'

'No. An abominable evening, sir. Do not let us misuse words. You are waiting for the mail coach?'

'Waiting for it? Not to misuse a word, sir, I am longing for it. Been here since three o'clock. Soaked to the marrow.'

'You'll be waiting till midnight. We passed it miles back. One wheel half off, two of the horses limping, a lady in hysterics, and the coachman drunk. Where are you going?'

'Pembroke. And me dinner. And a mustard bath.'

'Jump in!'

'Thankee. I'll come in, sir.'

Anthony pushes open the door and, puffing and squelching, Sir Henry enters the coach.

Anthony looks out of the window at the whirling dusk and the two dividing roads. He speaks to Sir Henry over his shoulder as he stares out.

'Quicker to go by the by-road?'

'If your springs'll stand it. It ain't a road by right, it's a lot o' holes strung together by ditches. Save you hours, if you live.'

Anthony calls through the window to the driver.

'Take the road on the left!'

And the driver's voice answers him through wind and rain, as if from a great distance.

'Yes, sir, yes, Mr Anthony. Road on the left.'

The driver is a very small man muffled up in soaking sacks and rugs. Only his eyes and his long cold nose are visible. He whips up the horses.

'Here we go . . .'

The chaise lurches violently.

'And we almost gone . . .'

From the box, we see the lurching lane. Down we go bumping into a series of holes and pits, and up come spraying waves of mud.

Inside the chaise, Anthony and Sir Henry sit opposite each other.

Anthony huddles deeper into his Army great-coat. He is a young man of quiet, almost mild, demeanour, slow to smile but with a shrewd intelligence and humour deceptively hidden by his air of rather studied nonchalance. His voice is cool.

Sir Henry is a stocky, plump, well-fed gentleman of middling age and rising blood pressure, fond of old port and old jokes. A gruff and canny vulgarian of the 'old school'. He fumbles inside his cloak.

'Got a hip-flask here. If I can find me hip. Haven't felt me *ribs* for years.'

He brings out a silver hip-flask of very generous proportions.

'Ah, here we are. Join me? No? Good health to you, Mister—?'

He ends his toast interrogatively, drinks, sits back, and removes his hat. A river of rain-water runs down over him.

'My name is Raine. Anthony Raine.'

Sir Henry looks up sharply at Anthony.

'Anthony Raine? Thought ye were in India. I knew your father well. Went to his funeral. Missed me breakfast. I'm Price-Parry.'

'Yes. Sir Henry.'

'Heard of me, eh? Don't tell me they know me in *India*. I've never been further than Boulogne myself. Sick four times – once going over, twice there and once coming back. Don't like foreigners. All deaf. Got to shout to make 'em understand.'

The chaise creaks, lurches and hiccups through the

mud and rain. Anthony shivers, huddles deeper in his coat.

'Is it always as wet as this in Wales?'

'Feeling the cold? That's bad. It's going to snow. I can tell – I've got a corn like a barometer. Almost as big, too . . . We thrive on the cold.'

'We, Sir Henry?'

'Me and Rover.'

A cat miaows, Anthony looks around him. Sir Henry chuckles.

'Come out, Rover . . .'

And a black cat puts his head out from inside Sir Henry's voluminous sodden cloak.

Anthony looks at it quizzically and in his mild, but slightly pedantic, way murmurs to Sir Henry:

'Rover's a dog's name.'

'It's a *dog* of a cat, sir. Ain't it, Rover?'

Rocking, the chaise slows up and stops. Anthony puts out his hand to lower the window.

'Tollgate.'

Anthony sighs. '*Another?*'

🦉     🦉     🦉

Out of the toll-house, the 'pike-man' advances towards the carriage, swinging a storm-lantern. He wears corduroy breeches, white stockings, white apron, and tall glazed hat. He looks up, grinning maliciously at the driver on the box, and speaks in a high whining voice.

'You been out in rain, you been!'

He jerks his head towards the closed chaise, leering.

'Who's inside 'er? Women?'

When he reaches the window of the chaise and peers inside, he mutters disgustedly to himself.

'Ach y fi!'

The window is lowered. Lewis looks over it and becomes immediately servile and, at the same time, knowing and familiar.

'Oh, its *you*, Sir Henry. Evening, Sir Henry. There's weather, Sir Henry! For ikkle fishes!'

He squints with sly curiosity at Anthony muffled in his corner.

'Evenin', other sir. Travelling far tonight?'

'Yes. And quickly.'

The pike-man remains unsnubbed.

'You got a new carriage, Sir Henry? Bought it in Carmarthen maybe? There's a nice town. My wife broke her leg in Carmarthen . . .'

Sir Henry cuts him short.

'The carriage belongs to this gentleman.'

'Oh! Then there is a shillin' toll to pay. Rules and regulations. Sir John Watkyn, M.P., come along here this mornin'. I tipped him the wink but "No" he says. "I'm payin' up like anyone else," he says. Keep his big gab shut he should in Parliament. Leave the tollgates alone he should, talkin' all nasty, when he could drive anywheres for nothin'.'

Anthony hands him a coin through the window.

'You may keep the change.'

The pike-man smiles, then looks at the coin in his hand.

'It's only a shillin' you give me.'

'Hm! So you can count!'

He raises the window.

Now outside on the muddy road, the chaise rattles and squelches past the pike-man, alone in the rain, still looking at the palm of his hand.

'Now there's a dishonest gentleman.'

Inside the chaise, Anthony gives Sir Henry a small smile.

'There's a rogue for you! He'd sell his mother for half an ounce of cats-meat.'

Sir Henry looks down at the cat in his lap, and, with a heavy jocoseness, shakes a warning finger at Anthony.

'Ssh! It understands English.'

But Anthony continues in his unruffled, nonchalant way, the rather violent words he uses in marked contrast to the almost priggish calmness of his voice.

'Every pike-man I've met at every tollgate on this vile road looks like a Welsh stoat that's been crossed with a spaniel – biting and fawning at the same time.'

Sir Henry strokes his cat with affection.

'Not a word against the Welsh, please – Rover comes from Aberystwyth.'

'And the number of those legalised highwaymen! These official pick-pockets! There must be more tollgates than liars in the country.'

'You're very peppery tonight, sir. I've always *heard* the Far East was bad for the liver. Mine stopped complaining long ago; it gave up the struggle. Oh, I agree with you, the pike-men are a naughty lot. Always a marvel to me how any toll-money gets into our pockets at all.'

Anthony glances at him politely, not understanding.

'*Our* pockets?'

Sir Henry darts a quick look at him.

'Oh, yes, of course. You've been away. But now

13

you're home, Mr Raine, you'll be learning a lot. Great things, these Turnpike Trusts. Very beneficial for the country.'

'For the *country*, Sir Henry?'

Sir Henry attempts to look conspiratorial, glances down at the bulge in his cloak and then up at Anthony.

'Well, between you and me and Rover, let us say – for *us*!'

🦉   🦉   🦉

The chaise rocking through the roaring wind and the almost-dark along a shining country road. The lights of lamps begin to appear in cottage and farmhouse windows at the roadside and in the wild-treed fields. The road grows more level. There are more and more lights flimmering out of the night. And the chaise pulls up outside a large, dark house.

The chaise door opens. Sir Henry steps out and calls back to Andrew:

'Good night – I beg your pardon, an abominable night. And many thanks. We must meet again.'

The cat puts out its nose and whiskers from Sir Henry's cloak, and miaows. From inside the carriage, Anthony calls:

'Good night, Sir Henry. Nice mice to you, Rover . . .' And then to the coachman 'Home, Dave, to Pentre House – and the quicker the better.'

The door closes and the chaise drives on through the rain.

The chaise drives past lodge and gates up a wide drive.

It pulls up outside Pentre House, lights in the lower windows.

The front door opens, and there, on the top step, framed against the warm and welcome light of the hall, stands Sara Jane Jones, the housekeeper, a fat, smiling, motherly woman dressed in austere black, chatelained, and with a high, white, frilled and cameo-brooched collar.

Anthony climbs out of the carriage and runs up the steps to Sara Jane.

'Master Anthony!'

He kisses her, and she holds him for a moment against her. Then she holds him out at arm's length and inspects him. She speaks with proprietorial, nanny-like no-nonsense briskness.

'Your feet are wet. You'll catch your death. Indoors you go! At once! Egg and hot milk for you.'

She calls out sternly to the little driver who is climbing, soaked, shivering and sorrowful, down from his box.

'Bring the bags in the hall, our Davy, and don't you dare drip on the carpets. . . . *In* you go, Master Anthony!'

And she bustles him inside, closing the door behind her.

🦉 🦉 🦉

Anthony, in an old dressing-gown and carpet-slippers, stands before the crackling log-fire in the drawing-room. He is looking with some apprehension at the glass in his hand. Sara Jones stands a little way from him, near the table on which a tray is set, looking at him with approval.

'Drink your milk now. You were always a boy for the milk . . . Drink it up!'

'Can I . . . have a drop of brandy in it?'

Sara Jane does not answer.

'Just a . . . little drop?'

'The cupboard's locked.'

'But you've got the key, Sara Jane.'

'I left it in my bedroom.'

'I can fetch it, Sara Jane Jones.'

'No man's ever been in my bedroom since the day Mr Jones, God rest him, got the quinsy in 1837 and never recovered. Amen . . . Now it's *off* to bed with you and don't forget your senna pods.'

Anthony sighs. 'How nice it is to be at home again Sara Jane – home and grown-up.'

'Grown-up indeed! Just because you've been a redcoat in heathen parts. But you should see Miss Rhiannon! No nonsense about *her* now, she's proper grown up! Called this afternoon with his lordship to ask when you were expected.'

'And what did you tell them?'

'I said you'd be round at Sarn Hall first thing in the morning – and mind you wipe your boots when you get there.'

'How is Lord Sarn?'

'The same as he always was – the most forgetful man in Pembrokeshire. Came down to dinner last week he did with his nightcap on. Said he thought it was Friday, but what that had to do with his wearing his nightcap at dinner nobody knows.'

'I saw Sir Henry Price-Parry tonight – he's a queer old stick'.

'Him and his black cat! When my grandmother was a girl, they'd a-burnt him for a he-witch.'

16

'He said he had something to do with the tollgates. Making a lot of money out of the Turnpike Trust, he said. What did he mean, Sara Jane?'

But Sara Jane suddenly becomes expressionless and when she speaks it is in a flat, toneless voice.

'I don't know about such things.'

She turns her back to him, pretending to straighten the curtains.

'But you always know everything that's happening.'

He moves away from the fire, down the oil-lamp lit drawing-room towards her, but Sara Jane keeps her back to him. She lifts a corner of the curtain and looks out into the night.

'I think it'll snow tomorrow.'

'There's nothing goes on in the countryside you don't know about,' persists Anthony.

'The farmers, they've been expecting snow.'

'Why won't you tell me? I only asked about the tollgates, Sara Jane.'

All this time he has been approaching her. Suddenly, abruptly, Sara Jane turns and leaves the room.

☙ ☙ ☙

Next morning, Anthony is standing, a heavy shawl about his shoulders, at the window, looking out on to the gardens and the drive and the lodge at the end covered with snow and the white fields, trees, hills and farmhouse beyond. Among distant trees tall house chimneys are to be seen. Snow is falling.

We see, from behind him, the snow-white landscape, hear him say:

'Good morning, Pentre Meadow . . . Argon Hill and David's Hill. There's Davy Button's cottage . . . And Evan the Thatcher's . . . like Christmas cards. And, yes, there's the chimneys of Sarn Hall, and over there in the trees . . .'

There is a knock on the door. Anthony half-turns around.

'Come in!'

Sara Jane comes in. She carries with her a pile of coats, greatcoats, scarves, shawls and rugs, which she dumps down on a chair.

'There! I told you there'd be snow this morning.'

'So did Sir Henry's corn.'

'I've brought you every warm piece of clothing in the house. You put them on at once before you catch your death! The sleigh's waiting.'

Anthony crosses to the heaped chair, lifts up one garment after the other, looks at them.

'Perhaps I've grown out of some of these . . . I'm quite a big boy now you know, Sara Jane.'

'Now don't you bother about appearances. You got to keep warm after all those Indian juggernauts and harems and goodness knows what else.'

Picking up an old-fashioned garment, Anthony asks, 'Must I really?'

'Now you hurry up. Davey's waiting. And his lordship, too, over at the Hall. And Miss Rhiannon.

And Sara Jane bustles out.

☺   ☺   ☺

Anthony comes out through the front door into the snow, muffled from top to foot, with a rug over his arm. All kinds and shapes of fur-collared coats and enormous driving capes seem to be enveloping him. On his head is a strange creation with massive ear-flaps, something between a balaclava and a deer-stalker.

Davy Button is waiting in the sleigh, the reins of the two horses in his hands. He looks up in amazement as Anthony comes, swaddled, down the steps towards him and calls briskly:

'Morning, our Davy.'

Davy makes a little, strangled noise in his throat, buries his face in his mufflers. Anthony looks at him suspiciously.

'Are you *laughing,* by any chance, Davy Button?'

Davy chokes in his muffler. 'I got the asthma.'

'Then you should *do* something about your asthma, Davy.'

He climbs into the sleigh. Davy slides the whip. The sleigh disappears down the drive.

The morning room of Sarn Hall looks out on to a white terrace and snow-sheeted gardens beyond. It is a large room and ornate, very much of the late Eighteenth Century. There are only a very few early-Victorian influences.

And Lord Sarn, seated in a deep chair near the great fire, is himself a late Eighteenth-Century figure. He is a long, thin, elderly, overbred aristocrat with a weak chin, a fine imperious nose, and a wandering air. His voice is gentle, unassuming, fluting. He phrases his periods with care, but often leaves his sentences in mid-air or loses them entirely.

Anthony sits on a couch near to him, his back to the open window and the snowscape. He has discarded some of his more voluminous over-capes and rugs, and, of course, his peculiar hat, but, even so, he appears to be embedded in clothes of many shapes, materials, and periods.

'And so, my dear boy,' says the fluting voice, 'when you become a Justice of the Peace, as your father, no doubt, would have wished, though he *was* such a very contrary fellow, God rest him, and become so violent about Lord Palmerston . . .'

His voice fades as he appears to notice, for the first time, Anthony's extensive overclothing.

'You feel the cold, I perceive. Shall I ring for a footwarmer?'

'Thank you, sir, I can wear *nothing* else.'

'You do not *wear* a footwarmer, Anthony, though perhaps in India there is some old tribal custom . . . Now, what was I saying? Ah, yes, Justice of the Peace.'

'I don't think I want to become a Justice of the Peace, sir.'

'Excellent! I'm glad that's settled. We will be meeting on the Bench this Thursday, my boy . . . Now, where's Rhiannon . . . ?'

He looks around the large room as if expecting her to come out of hiding.

'She *never* answers when I pull the bell.'

'Perhaps', suggests Anthony, rather hesitantly, 'because you haven't . . . er . . . pulled the bell.'

Lord Sarn looks at him sharply – then, as sharply,

pulls the bell rope. Anthony tries to fill the silence with a platitude . . .

'It's a long time since I was in this room. It's just the same.'

'Of course it is. Wouldn't know where I was if people kept changing things around.'

'The same carpets and chairs and pictures – even the same flower-vases.'

'They've changed the flowers, though, since you were here last.'

From across the room a voice asks: 'And am I the same?'

Anthony wheels round towards the door and, from his angle, we see Rhiannon standing at the open door, smiling. She is a very pretty girl of about twenty, charming, candid and self-possessed. She is dressed in outdoor clothes. Lord Sarn takes it on himself to answer her question, petulantly.

'Of course you're the same, Rhiannon. I saw you only half an hour ago. People do not change in that time, it is against nature.'

'I was asking Mr Raine, Uncle.'

'No, you're not the same,' Anthony tells her. 'But I would have known you. I can still see, I think, the pretty little girl I used to know, standing there and smiling behind the beautiful young lady I see now.'

Lord Sarn's voice breaks in, appreciatively.

'Very good. Who wrote that, my boy?'

Rhiannon tosses her proud head. 'I think perhaps you see only the surface of things, Mr Raine.'

'And do you remember far back enough to say whether *I* have changed?'

Rhiannon looks at him dispassionately, tilting her head.

'Yes, oh, yes. You're older, of course.'

'That is only to be expected.'

'And taller, too. And you've changed your shape. I mean, you *used* to have a shape and now . . .'

Lord Sarn rises to his full, thin, elegant height.

'Now, off with you both. This is no time or place to discuss the "shape" of young men. I must apologise to you, Anthony, for not being able to accompany you this morning . . .'

'Where am I going?' asks Anthony, surprised.

'You are going, very kindly, to drive me to Pembroke Market for my shopping' Rhiannon tells him, 'and on the way, I shall show you where all your tenants live.'

'But I know every acre and man in the place.'

'Things have changed. It isn't just you and I who aren't the same any more, Mr Raine. Shall we start?'

As she walks to the door, Lord Sarn rouses himself to say: '*How* I envy you your little drive. Bowling along in the crisp wintry weather. That's the life! Wish I could join you. Good day, my boy.'

Then, as Anthony leaves him, Lord Sarn sinks back into his deep chair, pulls it nearer the roaring fire, sighs contentedly, and reaches for the decanter.

᳕ ᳕ ᳕

Near the foot of the stairs stands a footman, straight-backed, still, and solemn, laden with Anthony's discarded scarves, coats and driving-cape.

Anthony comes out of the morning-room into the

hall, and the footman comes to life. Without expression he assists Anthony into his coats, one by one.

Rhiannon stops at the foot of the stairs, watching Anthony slowly disappearing under his winter layers, and asks: 'Are you sure you'll be warm enough?'

'Eh?'

'There's an old tent upstairs in the lumber-room. I think it would *just* go round you. And then you could light fire inside and roast chestnuts. Or would you like the tiger-skins off the library floor?'

'Thank you, no. There is no sense in *over*doing things. I am quite cosy now.'

He and Rhiannon go down the hall to the door. The footman watches them go, muttering to himself, flatly, expressionless, spacing the words out. 'He – is – quite – cosy, now.'

Anthony and Rhiannon walk together to where the sleigh and Davy Button are waiting. Rhiannon climbs into the sleigh.

'Don't drive too fast, our Davy. We all have to be so careful of Mr Raine's health, haven't we?'

Davy, his back to Anthony and Rhiannon, begins to croak and wheeze again. Anthony suggests mildly: 'I think our Davy's asthma needs attention. He makes a noise like bagpipes . . . Drive on, please.'

The sleigh moves down the drive.

      ☺      ☺      ☺

A snowbound country road, and white fields beyond, seen from the moving sleigh, across Anthony and Rhiannon.

Anthony stares at the snow and says, with dislike: 'Snow, snow, snow! Look at the beastly stuff!'

Rhiannon says, primly: 'If only we'd known of your arrival earlier, we could have postponed the snow. It was very remiss of us. You don't like the snow, Mr Raine?'

'Do *you* like the countryside laid out in white like a corpse? Birds starving, sheep lost and dying, chilblains, frostbite, pneumonia, ice in the washbasin, red noses. And every sentimentalist babbling about Old England, Chaucer's England, when snow *was* snow, as though Chaucer lived in a perpetual blizzard.'

'You read poetry as well, Mr Raine?'

'Even soldiers read.'

'But you aren't a soldier any more. You're a squire. You're a land-owner. You are one of the landed gentry.'

Now they are passing a group of small dilapidated cottages. At the door of one of them stands a peasant woman and three small children. Rhiannon nudges Anthony.

'Lift your hat to your happy, smiling tenants, Mr Raine.'

Anthony raises his peculiar headwear and waves to the little group at the door.

'Good morning, Mrs Griffiths!'

The woman and the children make no response to his salutation, but stare at the sleigh dully and suspiciously.

'Perhaps they don't like the hat.'

Though his words are facetious, his tone is puzzled and a little hurt.

The windows of the next cottage they pass are boarded up. It is in very bad repair, and obviously empty. Rhiannon glances sideways at Anthony.

'Perhaps they're ungrateful enough not to like

living in pig sties. Perhaps they don't like being bullied and cheated at every one of your tollgates.'

'Not mine, I assure you!'

Rhiannon takes no notice of his interjection.

'So that you and all the members of your Trust can build fine roads to your houses and buy new horses and carriages and drink yourselves under the tables every night.'

'I assure you, alcohol is poison to me.'

'Of course. I was forgetting. You must take care of your health.'

'Well, *do* you want me to drink, or don't you?'

'I don't care if you clean your teeth in brandy, Mr Raine.'

Anthony shakes his head at her, gravely. 'That would be very bad for the enamel.'

&#9775;   &#9775;   &#9775;

Now, as they move along the country road, they see, some way in front of them, a solitary farm-labourer. He steps towards the hedge as the sleigh approaches. Anthony waves to him as they pass and calls: 'Hullo to you, Shoni Fawr!'

The man does not look up. The sleigh passes him. He stares after it, spits, and goes off, crunching through the snow, in the opposite direction.

'I really must have changed a lot. He didn't recognise me.'

'I think he did.'

'Then why didn't he say hullo?'

'*Because* he recognised you.'

Anthony looks at her with a puzzled expression, but she is staring at the countryside, passing.

☙ ☙ ☙

When Anthony and Rhiannon drive up to the St Clears tollgate, they find their road blocked by baaing sheep. William Evans, a very old farmer, is arguing fiercely with Jack Wet, the pike-man, a most unprepossessing fellow with low forehead, brutal features, and little piggish eyes.

'I'm not paying a penny to any boosy blackguard with a shiny hat and a fancy apron. The sheep went up the mountain by themselves.'

'And they come down on *this* side of the gate through a 'ole in the 'edge. If you want 'em to go back through this gate, you pay, William Evans. Or you can drive 'em back the way they came.'

The old farmer shakes with fury. 'How can I do that? I haven't got my dog. He's sick, I told you.'

'He's been eating Mrs Evans's cooking. Get down on all fours and *bark* yourself then, grandpa. The sheep won't know.'

'You're a thief and a sot, Jack Wet, and a billygoat and a blasphemer and you've always been so ever since you was a boy, all pimples and fleas.'

Jack Wet spits contemptuously. 'You're too old to live, you old corpse, you should 'ave been buried. You're cheating the undertaker.'

26

'*You* can talk of burials. Who got drunk at his Aunty Dosie's funeral and fell on his head in the grave-hole? Who puts dirty buttons on the collection plate? Who gives his Morged a black eye every Saturday night?'

The tollgate man is not to be outdone. 'Who's an old miser? Who waters his milk? Whose daughter run away to Fishinguard with a deaf barber?'

'You leave my Polly out of it. And he wasn't a barber either, he was a . . .'

'You pay the toll. How many sheep?'

'I don't pay nothing. Three score.'

'Three score. Penny a head. Five shillings.'

William Evans, in a terrible indignation, addresses his sheep with oratorical fervour and wavings of his arms.

'Listen to that, listen to that, will you! Five shillings! And it used to be twopence halfpenny a score.'

Jack Wet takes a list from his pocket and hands it to him.

'Not on this turnpike. Here, look for yourself.'

'I can't read.'

'Nor me. But there it is, in black and white. *Five shillings!*'

'May your father rise out of the quicklime in Carmarthen Jail and . . .'

He stops suddenly, his anger vanishing and his face brightening as he sees Rhiannon, Anthony and Davy in the halted sleigh. He goes across and hands the toll-list to Rhiannon.

'Miss Rhiannon! *You're* a scholar, Miss Rhiannon. Will you spell this for me?'

But Anthony puts out his hand and takes the toll-list.

'Here, let me see.'

'Penny a head for my sheep, this polecat says.'

Jack Wet appears at the old man's side.

'I'll have the law on you. Calling me a polecat.'

Anthony, meanwhile, is looking down the list.

'Cattle, pigs, horses, donkeys, goats, all the menagerie. Here we are. Sheep. Penny a head.'

The old man looks at him suspiciously. 'Is that what it says?'

Anthony looks up at him. 'You're William Evan *Dolcoed,* aren't you? Do you remember me?

'I knew a young lad once fron Pentre Hall. But he wouldn't have grown to tell an old man lies. He was a good boy.'

Rhiannon has taken the list from Anthony.

'Mr Raine isn't lying, Evan. He should know his own charges. Yes, penny a head.'

'I told you,' says Jack Wet, righteously, 'but you wouldn't believe me.'

The old man touches his cap. 'Thank yer, Miss Rhiannon . . . I wouldn't believe *you,* Jack Wet, if you signed the pledge on your deathbed.'

He brings out an old purse, and, together, he and Jack Wet move away, still arguing. Anthony appeals to Rhiannon.

'Would you belive *me* if I said that I have had nothing in the world to do with – this?'

He touches the list, with distaste.

'No.'

'These prices – they're mad!'

'Yes.'

'People like old Evan *can't* pay them.'

'They do. They have to.'

28

Davy joins in, without turning round from his driver's seat.

'In Carmarthen there have been riots. Tollgates on fire and houses pulled down and pikemen thrown whoosh! in the pond.' He adds, with relish, 'Very sinful'.

'No riots here?'

There is a note of regret in Davy's voice as he answers, 'Not yet, sir, no.'

And the same note in Rhiannon's voice, as she adds, 'Nobody has the courage to start them.'

Jack Wet comes back to the sleigh unpleasantly cheerful. He holds out his hand to Anthony.

'Now your turn. A shilling please.'

Anthony looks at the list.

'Coach, carriage with four horses, carriage with – no, there's no mention of a sleigh. Only of carriages with wheels.'

'We got no wheels,' puts in Davy.

Jack Wet is flummoxed. 'Is that what the writing says? No wheels, no charge?'

Anthony and Rhiannon nod their heads gravely, and Anthony orders: 'Open the gate!'

Jack Wet goes off grumbling. 'It don't make no sense. Sheep got no wheels neither.'

Rhiannon looks across at Anthony. 'I'm glad you did that.'

'I'm glad you liked me doing it. What is that brute's name?'

Davy from the driver's seat supplies the answer: 'They call him Jack Wet. Cos he's always got his nose in a pint-pot.'

'I'll remember him . . . Drive on, Davy, drive on. If

you smell any brimstone, it's me – I'm the devil to-day.'

And the sleigh drives on through the open tollgate, Jack Wet watching it pass with a face full of resentment.

☺    ☺    ☺

From the driver's seat of a smart carriage drawn up in the centre of Pembroke Market, Sir John Watkyn, M.P. is addressing a crowd. He is a young man of energy and persuasion, but one inclined to fall back on to compromise when confronted by any positive issue. And he is apt to be infatuated by his own oratory. The voices of the crowd, raised in anger and indignation, fade to a murmuring as Sir John speaks.

'Shame!' you cry. "Shame on the Tollgate system", and I lend my voice to yours.'

From the back of the crowd a voice yells: 'Lend us your carriage, mun!'

Sir John tries again. '"Shame", I cry with you. Shame on these iniquities that go by the name of law –'

In the foremost section of the crowd is a young farmer, Rhodri Huws, with a bunch of his cronies. He shouts: 'What's sacred about the law?'

And one of his cronies, Owen Owen, adds his interjection: 'Constable Morgan got a halo then?'

Sir John is not to be heckled, but carries on: 'And away, I say, with the levelling of exorbitant charges so that a small minority may profit. So far I go with you, but *you* cry, "Violence", and *I* say "Mediation". *You* cry, "We will take into our own hands the destruction of this barbarous

30

system". And *I* say, "the removal of these iniquities *must* come by constitutional means".'

Anthony and Rhiannon's sleigh drives into the square and draws up at the back of the crowd as Sir John finishes speaking. The crowd begins to shout, some in approval, others, led by Rhodri Huws, in open hostility.

'Pull the tollgates down!'

'What's stopping us!'

'Law and order!'

'They charges you for a barrow-load o' dung!'

'Throw them in it!'

'Why was the Reform Bill passed?'

Rhodri Huws answers the last question.

'Because the Government was afraid of a Revolution.'

During this, Anthony and Rhiannon leave the sleigh and make their way along the outskirts of the crowd, getting nearer to Rhodri Huws and his supporters. Anthony is looking about him with considerable interest. He questions a stout red-faced farmer next to him, nodding in Rhodri's direction.

'Who's that? Over there.'

'That's Rhodri Huws. Always argufying!'

Another farmer, a sharp little man, joins in.

'Pick a quarrel with an echo he would! Trouble raiser!'

And a third – 'Seen him fighting three tinkers at once. Bang, bang, there's fisticuffs! Blood all over the shop, like a choir outing!'

'On a Sunday too.'

Quietly to Rhiannon, Anthony admits: 'I like the look of him.'

One of Rhodri's supporters has, with a nudge, directed

Rhodri's attention to Anthony. And Rhodri looks at him with an expression of angry contempt.

Rhiannon notes it. 'But he doesn't seem to like the look of you.'

Anthony pays no attention, but asks: 'Who was the speaker?'

The farmers are delighted to inform him. 'Sir John Watkyn' – and then with great reverence – 'M.P.!'

And their companion adds, rolling the words with relish – 'A redoubtable rhetorician.'

Rhiannon and Anthony move on. They are walking side by side through the snow, Anthony huddled in his coats, when voices are heard raised angrily. Rhiannon stops and turns. 'They're following us.'

'Who?' asks Anthony, unconcernedly.

He turns also. Coming towards him is a small group of farm-labourers, led by Rhodri Huws.

Anthony smiles. 'Ah! The trouble raiser! "Bang, bang, blood all over the shop." Not mine, I hope.'

Rhodri Huws approaches, his face hard and set. He stares at Anthony menacingly.

'I wanted to see you close.'

Anthony returns his gaze. 'I trust I improve on inspection?'

'I wanted to see what a young *bloodsucker* looked like.'

'Just like an old one, I should think. Only less wrinkled.'

'I wanted to see an *officer and a gentleman* face to face, who comes home to his estates and the money he never earned a penny piece of, to sneer and swindle the poor and set himself above other men.'

Coolly, Anthony addresses Rhiannon who, standing

near, is pale and angry. "I am almost persuaded I *do* smell of brimstone. What a devil I am, to be sure.'

A voice from the group behind Huws urges: 'Give him brimstone, Rhodri!'

There is a second's pause. Then Anthony asks: 'Well, having seen me close?'

Rhodri steps back from him, contemptuously. 'I was going to knock you down, but now I wouldn't touch you.'

The same voice from the crowd urges: 'Kick him in the bread basket, Rhodri!'

Anthony smiles coolly at Huws. 'I'm glad of that. And now, gentlemen, like your manners, I must leave you. Good-day, Mr Rhodri Huws.'

'You know my name. You'll hear it again, soon enough, Mr Magistrate.'

Rhiannon has turned away. Anthony hurries after her and takes her lightly by the arm, but she frees herself and looks at him with cold scorn and disgust. Anthony appears not to notice her emotions.

'Did you hear that? "Mr Magistrate". The things he called me.'

'Oh, you're a *coward,* Anthony Raine!'

She speaks in a fury of loathing. Anthony appears unperturbed. 'The things *you* call me too.'

'To see you standing there, *listening* to him *insult* you, never lifting a *finger* for yourself.'

Anthony, in deprecation, raises his many-mitted hands and demonstrates. 'Couldn't find a finger to lift.'

'Oh, you wouldn't say "Bo" to a goose!'

'Of course I wouldn't. What an absurd thing to say to a goose . . . Besides, I liked Rhodri Huws. I shall look forward to seeing him again.'

Without a word, Rhiannon turns from him and walks quickly down the snowy Market Square. Anthony follows, keeping pace with her. 'I do hope there is a woollen stall in the market. I should like to buy some bed-socks.'

Rhiannon's back stiffens. The scene fades.

⊕    ⊕    ⊕

Pembroke Magistrate's Court is in session. The body of the Court is filled with farmers and farm-labourers and small tradesmen, among who we recognise some of Rhodri's supporters and the farmers Anthony questioned in the market place.

Standing in the dock is Rhodri Huws, guarded by a parish constable. And on the magistrates' bench sits Anthony, still heavily clad, next to Lord Sarn who is Chairman. There are two other magistrates. The clerk sits below the bench.

In the witness-box, a pike-man in uniform, is giving evidence. 'Up he comes with his horse and cart and I say to him, polite, "Will you have the goodness, Mr Huws" I say, "to pay the small matter of a sixpence toll". And he jumps off the cart with his whip in his hand and he says – Do you want me to repeat the exact words he used, Your Honours?'

Lord Sarn immediately says 'Yes, yes!', but the two other smug and whiskered magistrates gravely shake their heads and the clerk leans up to whisper. Lord Sarn changes his verdict to 'No, no!' The Pike-man proceeds cautiously: 'He says "I'll be blowed if I will", he says, though that wasn't the word he used, you understand. And then he casts aspersions.'

Lord Sarn pounces. 'Did he? On whom?'

The Pike-man continues placidly. 'On me and my father and grandfather and Sir Henry Price-Parry and on the Board of Magistrates and you yourself, sir, and the Government and my wife who happened to poke her nose out of the window.'

Lord Sarn is enjoying himself hugely, but trying not to show it. 'A very comprehensive selection. And then?'

'Then he says, "You let me through, or I'll . . ." And he says what he'll do to me if I don't. So I don't want him to do that to me, do I? So I lets him through.'

An anti-climax. Lord Sarn rouses himself sufficiently to ask Rhodri if he has anything to say. When Rhodri says 'Yes', he murmurs to Anthony: 'I was afraid he would,' and adds in his official voice: 'Will you make your statement from the witness-box?'

Rhodri answers coolly: 'No. I can tell the truth from here or anywhere. I object to the presence of one of the magistrates.'

A loud stir in the court-room. Lord Sarn is heard to murmur with relief to Anthony: 'Good! Perhaps I can go home then.' But one of the other magistrates insists: 'Who does he object to?'

The Clerk repeats the question and Rhodri replies: 'Mr Anthony Raine, who makes money out of the tollgates!'

The muttering in court rises. Lord Sarn lifts his little chairman's hammer and says to Anthony. 'This is the only part I like.'

And he bangs the hammer down. Silence. Lord Sarn leans over to the Clerk, who rises. 'What the deuce do we do now?' he asks. 'Can I fine him yet?'

'No, no, sir,' says the Clerk in a desperate whisper: 'I am afraid he must be allowed to make his defence.'

35

Lord Sarn smiles. He is on firm ground again. 'Of course, of course. And *then* I fine him. I rather like that part, too. Proceed with the case.'

The Clerk whispers again. 'And I'm afraid that he is within his rights. He can object if a magistrate might in any way be prejudiced. Perhaps if Mr Raine would – er – just for a moment . . . under the circumstances . . .'

Anthony gets up at once. 'Certainly, certainly! With the greatest pleasure.'

He goes out. Lord Sarn looks at his departing back and muses sadly: 'Nobody objects to me.' Then he turns to Rhodri and barks. 'Well?'

Rhodri states his case. 'My cart was empty. I took it to the quarry to get lime for my land. And I *paid* when I brought it back loaded. That tollgate has been put up near the quarry on purpose to catch us and make us pay twice. I refused *then,* and I refuse *for ever.*'

'That is a most improper suggestion on your part,' Lord Sarn tells him. Then he calls to the Clerk 'What's the position here? Eh, eh?'

'The exemption claimed by the defendant seems to be in respect of dung brought from town.'

'But lime is not dung!' points out a magistrate. Lord Sarn agrees: 'Very true, sir, very true!'

'In foreign countries it's allowed,' Rhodri tells him.

'What foreign countries?'

'England.'

A titter runs round the courtroom. Lord Sarn bangs his hammer. Above the noise, Rhodri shouts to make himself heard. 'All our lives we pay. We pay you rents and rates and you let us live in hovels and never mend the roads we use. We pay to live and we are always poor. We live to pay and keep *you* rich by our work. And now you put up toll-gates so that we have to pay to *work*.'

And the murmur of the court crowd rises. Lord Sarn bangs his hammer again, but this time the crowd will not be silenced.

⠀⠀⠀⠀⠀☾⠀⠀⠀☾⠀⠀⠀☾

The risen murmuring of the court can be heard in the background. A parish constable stands at the closed court-room door. Anthony, waiting in the dark, chill passage, stamps his feet, beats his hands together. Sir Henry Price-Parry comes in and greets him heartily.

'Still cold, still cold? Tell me, my boy, how many waistcoats d'you wear?'

'If I numbered them alphabetically, this morning I'd be up to M,' admits Anthony.

'Have some brandy. Gives you a kind of waistcoat inside, with little hard buttons on.'

Anthony shakes his head. 'No, thank you. Alcohol is poison to me.'

Sir Henry grimaces and takes a huge swig from his hip-flask. 'An irreligious thought . . . Ah, that's better. I'm beautifully poisoned now.'

'And how is Rover this morning?'

'Indisposed. I left him at home with a splitting headache. Why aren't you on the bench? Trying that ruffian Huws, aren't they? Wish they'd hang him.'

'He objected to my presence on the bench. He said that I made money out of the tollgates.'

37

'Well, so you do, don't you?'

'Do I?'

'Of *course* you do. What did you think would happen when your father died? We naturally elected you to his place on the trusts. All you've got to do is to sit on your breeches once a month at a committee meeting. How many pairs of *them* do you wear, I wonder?'

☺ ☺ ☺

Through a door with a new brass plate inscribed 'WHITLAND TURNPIKE TRUST', we move in silence down a corridor to another door marked 'STRICTLY PRIVATE'. We move on to a notice that says 'SILENCE', and then to another door on which is pinned a notice saying 'COMMITTEE IN SESSION'. From behind the door comes loud laughter and the clinking of glasses and bottles. We go inside.

Six trustees, including Sir Henry Price-Parry, his cat on his lap, and Anthony next to him, recline in various attitudes of leisurely comfort, at a long table on which are decanters and glasses. Each trustee, except Anthony, has a glass before him, or in his hand, or at his lips. They are all, except Anthony, full of bonhomie and spirits. But Anthony, nearest the log fire, and still heavily clothed, sits glassless and miserable.

The first trustee, Mr Pugh, an ancient little man with a big Punch-like nose and a red-rimmed eye, is finishing a story. 'And that was that, and I tiptoed out of the room in my stockinged feet and climbed through the window and

38

down the ivy and I never saw her again, upon me word.'

'You never climbed *up* the ivy again?' asks his neighbour.

'Never again, I swear.'

'You're a gay deceiver, Mr Pugh.'

'Ah, but that was a long time ago. Young women are different nowadays, eh, Mr Raine?'

He winks at Anthony, who replies: '*All* women terrify me, sir.'

'And alcohol is poison' adds Sir Henry gloomily. 'Shall we turn to business, gentlemen? Now you've all studied the plans and I think it needn't take us long.'

Anthony looks up from his papers. 'Excuse me, Sir Henry. I have so little experience, of such matters as these. But it seems that there are *seven* tollgates on this road already.

Across the table, one of the other trustees remarks: 'It's a road the farmers find particularly convenient to use on market days, sir.'

'And to put up *three* new tollgates will of course add greatly to its convenience.'

'Excellently put, sir!' giggles Pugh. He guffaws uproariously.

Anthony waits for the merriment to subside and goes on: 'If you will bear with me a moment more. I understand also that this road is in extremely bad condition. Does that mean that the tolls taken at the gates already in existence are not enough to maintain it? And would it be true to say that a turnpike trust, therefore, is not profitable?'

The members begin to exchange dubious glances.

'You will appreciate, gentlemen, that I have been abroad for some years and am not familiar with these prob-

39

lems. I ask only for enlightenment.'

Two of the other trustees swiftly provide it. 'It is precisely to *make* it profitable, sir, that we are putting up these three additional gates.'

'Which are, of course, indispensable.'

Anthony sits back and smiles at them guilelessly. 'Of course. Thank you. I understand perfectly now. How simple business is, once one grasps the essentials.' He suddenly shivers. 'Do you find that the temperature of the room has been going down steadily?'

'No. I thought it was getting rather hotter.'

'Then perhaps I am catching a chill.'

'Do you feel shivers down your back?'

'Yes I do.'

'And a kind of tickle in the nostrils, like a feather?'

Anthony nods.

'And a humming in the ears?'

Anthony nods again. Sir Henry sums up. 'Then if I were you, I should wrap up well and go home at once!'

Mr Pugh adds solicitously: 'Get by your own fireside with a hot drink,' but Sir Henry puts him right. 'No, no! No poison!'

'A hot *milk* drink,' Mr Pugh corrects himself.

Anthony has risen and is struggling into his topcoats. 'Thank you. I will take your advice.'

He goes to the door and stands there looking at the trustees.

'Either I am contracting a severe chill or something has disagreed with me. Why even as I look at you now, I feel a distinct sense of nausea.' He puts on his preposterous hat. 'Excuse me, gentlemen. Good-day.'

He goes out, leaving behind a babble of speculation.

'How ingenuous *is* that young man?' asks one of the trustees.

'Oh, altogether. You can see he's a pampered pet.'

'A mollycoddling hypochondriac.'

'*Doesn't drink!*'

'Frightened of the women!'

'Boy's a fool!'

Sir Henry again sums up. 'Well, he won't trouble us again. Not in this weather. Let's hope it lasts.'

He pushes the box of cigars across the table, and lights his own.

🜨   🜨   🜨

Sunday morning. The bell of Bethel Chapel is ringing. In twos and threes, the congregation comes walking down the wintry lanes and enters the chapel.

Up in her boudoir at Sarn House, Rhiannon sits in front of the mirror, surveying the final results of her toilette. Reflected in the mirror is Bessy, her maid, who is holding an outdoor coat and bonnet. The chapel bell sounds in the distance. Rhiannon inspects them and says: 'Yes, those will do, Bessy.'

Bessy lays the coat and bonnet nearby, and kneels down to help Rhiannon put her little furred boots on.

'Is Captain Marsden here yet?'

'Oh yes, miss. He's been here quite a while.' She tries to suppress a delighted giggle. 'Mr Raine's here, too, miss.'

'Indeed? When did he arrive?'

41

'Just now, miss. Says he hopes to have the pleasure of accompanying you to chapel.'

Down below, in the hall, Anthony, swathed as before, is waiting. He turns to see Captain Marsden come out of the morning-room, resplendent in dragoon's uniform. The Captain is an impressive young man, handsome, stiff-backed, self-conscious, with a deep voice and a stern, uncompromising expression. He sees Anthony and stares with amazement at his superabundant costume, but soon regains his air of customary hauteur.

'Good day to you, sir.'

'Good day to you.'

'May I present myself? Marsden my name—on detachment here.'

'Anthony Raine, at your service.'

'Lord Sarn has mentioned you. Been serving abroad, I believe?'

'Yes.'

'India?'

'Yes.'

'Hot there.'

'Very.'

'Cold here.'

'Very.'

'Attending divine service?'

'That is my intention.'

'Mine too. By kind invitation of Miss Rhiannon.'

'And I—*not* by kind invitation of Miss Rhiannon.'

'Indeed?'

'Indeed. I shall attend divine service nevertheless.'

'I see.'

'No objection to that, I take it, sir?'

'On my part, sir, no.'

'No?'

'No.'

From above them comes Rhiannon's voice. 'What *are* you two talking about?'

And both men turn round quickly to see Rhiannon coming down the staircase towards them.

'Captain Marsden and I have been making friends. We have so much in common.'

'I am delighted to hear it. I gather you are coming to church with us, Mr Raine?'

Lord Sarn, appearing at the top of the stairs, corrects her: 'No, my dear, *chapel*. To-day, for a special reason, we attend the—er—*other* place of worship.'

Rhiannon looks at him suspiciously. 'Have you been quarrelling with the rector again?'

'Quarrelling? I am on the most *cordial* terms with that insufferable numbskull. No, there is a very special reason. I shall, no doubt, remember it later.'

They move down the hall to the front door, Marsden as stiff as a poker and ostentatiously as far away from Anthony as possible.


☙   ☙   ☙


The congregation of Bethel Chapel is on its feet, singing a Welsh hymn, as Lord Sarn's party come in. Many surprised, disapproving and enquiring glances are turned in their direction. The hymn finishes, and the congregation sits down. Then Mordecai Thomas, the preacher, mounts into the high pulpit. He is a thin, ardent man of middle age, with fiery deep-set eyes and a shock of wild, black hair. An hour-glass stands on the pulpit before him. He looks down at Lord Sarn and begins. 'To-day, my friends, the preaching will be in English, and for this reason—there are strangers among us. Not strangers to our daily lives, but to this, our humble house. To them we speak a strange and foreign tongue. Therefore will we speak in the tongue which is theirs. And therefore will be bold, as is commanded in the Scriptures, and speak to them what is in our hearts. For who knows but that they have seen the error of their ways and have come among us to worship and repent.'

'Hallelujah,' says Beth Morgan, fervently from her seat in the front row.

All eyes are now on Lord Sarn and his party, sitting awkward and embarrassed among the congregation of small farmers, tradesmen and their wives, in the severe, bare chapel. Children stare wide-eyed at the sight of Marsden in his splendid uniform and Anthony in his host of coats. Anthony and Marsden stare without expression directly before them at the preacher in the pulpit, Rhiannon between them, and sensing their hostility, glances swiftly up at each in turn. Lord Sarn looks cautiously around him at the congregation. A small boy, with a suspicious swelling in the cheek, catches Lord Sarn's eye and hastily gulps. The swelling vanishes. The small boy looks away.

Mordecai Thomas has opened the big Bible. He turns the hour-glass over and begins. 'My text is taken from Genesis, the twenty-fourth chapter and the sixtieth verse. And they blessed Rebecca and said unto her, "Thou art our sister. Be thou the mother of thousands of millions, and let thy seed possess *the gate of those that hate them*." I ask

44

you now—*What* are "the gates"? And *who* are they that keep the gates and that hate Rebecca and her seed? And Rebecca and her seed, who are they among us? It is not revealed to us whether Abraham, Isaac and Jacob paid toll to their enemies at these gates, but it is very sure that the gates were an oppression and an abomination, as are the gates upon the roads of the land wherein we labour. Consider now these gates, and the enemy at the gates and the blessed Rebecca and her seed who shall possess them. . .'

The sands are running down in the hour-glass.

☙ ☙ ☙

Outside the chapel, on the box of the Sarn carriage, the coachman is fast asleep, his head sunk on his chest. He moves uncomfortably in his sleep and snores with his elbow against the woodwork of the box. He mutters in his sleep, crossly, in a drowsy whisper 'Move up! Move up, Mary Ann! Always taking all the covers!'

He elbows his invisible sleeping-partner with so much force he wakes with a sharp groan. He feels his elbow, tenderly. From the chapel comes the droning of the preacher's voice.

The sands are lower in the hour-glass now. But Mordecai Thomas is still speaking . . .

'We pay toll at these gates when we travel the roads about our lawful business. And where does the money go? Are the roads kept in repair for those that use them and pay for them out of their poverty? No, they are muckheaps and ruins that wreck our carts and cripple our horses and cattle.

Where does the money go that is dragged out from our poverty? It is lost among the riches of the enemy at the gate. Let us now pray for a deliverer that shall be raised up among us, so that the seed of Rebecca, Rebecca's daughters, shall indeed possess the gates of her enemies and *lay them low*!'

He closes the Bible in front of him with a thud.


&#x2982;     &#x2982;     &#x2982;


The congregation is coming out at last. The group from Sarn House walks towards its carriage, watched covertly by the rest of the congregation, whispering among themselves. Captain Marsden falls in alongside Lord Sarn. 'Well, my lord, now you've got all the evidence you want. Sheer sedition, nothing less.'

'But why did it take so long?' his lordship asks, petulantly. 'Three hours! Where's that damned carriage? I'm famished.'

Rhiannon is about to follow him into the carriage when Betti Morgan steps up to her and presses a tract into her hand.

'Pray for forgiveness,' she says 'for the sinfulness of your bonnet. Please take this.'

Rhiannon looks in astonishment at the tract in her hand; then gets into the carriage, followed by the others. Her uncle settles himself among the rugs and says: 'I remember now, *that's* why I went to that Calvanistic ice house to-day—to hear this preacher—what's his name?'

The gallant captain supplies it: 'Mordecai Thomas. I'd have the fellow transported.'

46

'But what has this biblical woman, Rebecca, to do with it all? And as for her seed! . . . Home, Edwards, quick as you can. I want me dinner.'

Across the carriage, Marsden persists: 'Quite clearly he was encouraging the farmers to violence, sir.'

And Lord Sarn gently corrects him: 'Not farmers, no. Rebecca's seed.'

'If I were a farmer,' says Anthony, quietly, 'I should say he was right.'

Rhiannon turns to him at once. 'You say that! *You*!'

'*If* I were a farmer I should detest the tollgates. And I'd be inclined to possess the gates and lay them low.'

Marsden picks this up at once. 'And if you were a farmer and the militia were called in, I should see that you were flogged and jailed.'

'But as you are not a farmer, Mr Raine?'

'I shall go home and forget the whole thing. Including Captain Marsden and his floggings . . . Do you take your whip to bed, sir? It should be good company for your spurs.'

Lord Sarn looks at Marsden with interest. He puts his hand on the gallant captain's knee and says confidentially: 'Don't you find spurs tear the sheets?'

Meanwhile, Rhiannon is looking contemptuously at Anthony. 'I should have known better,' she whispers. 'Your *blood* is cold, too.'

And the carriage goes away, swaying and jolting down the rough, rutted road.

☙        ☙        ☙

It is a very muddy lane, but the day is bright, sunny and snowless. A cottage stands on the boggy roadside and outside this cottage workmen are putting up a new toll-gate.

On the far side of the gate is a large farm wagon loaded with two more gates. And from this side of the gate, a group of farmers, a dozen or so, including Rhodri Huws, Old William Evans, Shoni Fawr, and several of Rhodri's supporters whom we have seen before, are watching the men at work. The new pikeman stands at the cottage door and watches the workmen and the farmers. Some of them are jeering at the workmen, who take no notice, but stubbornly work on.

'Look at that one. The hairy one with the hammer.'

'I seen him in a cage at the fair.'

'Give him a nut!'

'They must have squoze that one in the gate, mun!'

He draws attention to a very thin workman. And some of the farmers laugh jeeringly. Rhodri Huws turns on them.

'That's right, boys. Laugh your wooden heads off. You won't be laughing on market day. Go on, fill your eyes. You won't be filling your bellies now.'

William Evans agrees, shaking his head. 'That's the *tenth* gate on this road. And two more to go up.'

The pikeman moves from his cottage door to inspect the new gate with a proprietorial smile. He swings the gate, tentatively.

The farmers discuss him.

'Look at that greasy barrel smiling there,'

'Throw him through the windy.'

'I'd like to cut him another smile with a billhook.'

'Shove him up his chimbley, I say.'

Rhodri Huws breaks in, savagely. 'Go on, break his bones for him! Stuff him with scum! Toss him on your pitchforks, you clods! What'll you get out of it? D'you think it will stop the gates? D'you think it'll stop Sir Henry Price-Parry, Anthony Raine Esquire and the rest from carrying on till there's more gates than cowsheds in the county?'

The farmers have turned away from the gate. The pikeman beckons towards the cottage, and his wife and small daughter come out. They all look at the gate. And the farmers grumble.

'What'll we do then?'

'Pay the toll and sing hymns?'

'Kiss the nice pikeman?'

Old William Evans suggests dubiously: 'We could ask Sir John Watkyn again.'

And Rhodri Huws cuts him short. 'Members of Parliament – pah!' He spits. 'They set up committees where they should set up gallows! Go on, ask your London Liberal gabbler to get down on his knees and plead for us . . . You might as well ask that little brat over there, for all the good it'll do . . . Sir John Watkyn indeed!'

The pikeman's little daughter is swinging on the new tollgate as the group of grumbling farmers move off.

☙     ☙     ☙

In the boardroom of the Turnpike Trust, Sir John Watkyn, M.P. is standing stiffly and seriously at the foot of the table, facing the trustees. There is Sir Henry Price-Parry, cat on lap, Anthony, Mr Pugh and the other trustees we have seen before. Also at the table, some little way from the trustees, sits Lord Sarn. And Captain Marsden stands behind him.

Anthony is at last unmuffled, but appears bored and abstracted. He does not look up when Sir John asks 'And your answer gentlemen?'

Sir Henry is having trouble with his blood-pressure. 'Our answer is amazement, sir. You have taken away our breath.'

And Mr Pugh adds grimly: 'But you won't take away our gates.'

Sir Henry clears his throat. 'I'm not a man that's *easily* amazed, sir . . .'

The ancient Punch-like Pugh leers and winks. 'Ha! I could amaze ye, Henry!'

'. . . by the crackpot idealism of young politicians just out of napkins. But your little taradiddle . . .'

Lord Sarn quietly repeats 'Taradiddle' to himself as if it were a word in a nursery rhyme . . . 'Taradiddle . . .' Sir Henry completes his sentence—

'. . . fairly flummoxes me,' and turns his purple attention to Mr Pugh. 'Neither am I amazed at the reminiscences of octagenarian libertines, Mr Pugh.'

'It's a lie! Seventy one.'

Lord Sarn shakes his head. 'The *words* he uses! Octagenarian! Taradiddle!'

'It's his blood-pressure, your lordship, it goes to his vocabulary.'

Sir Henry plunges on. 'All this moonshine and poppycock about the tollgates – lack a'daisy.' He breaks off

50

for want of other words to express his amazement and incredulity.

Mr Pugh turns to Sir John. 'You seriously mean to tell us that unless we remove the new gates and lower the toll charges of the others, there'll be a revolution in the county? I don't believe you.'

And the trustees around the table murmur 'Never! Revolution? Poo!'

Sir John tries again, patiently. 'What I was trying to say, gentlemen, was that, in my opinion, the situation might easily lead to open disorder. There is no police force in the county.'

'But there *is* Captain Marsden,' points out one of the trustees. 'Any trouble – and I don't believe for a moment there will be any – and down he comes.'

Anthony adds quietly: 'Spurs, whip and all!'

Marsden picks him up angrily: 'I resent your attitude.'

'And I,' says Sir Henry, 'resent the fact that we have wasted a whole afternoon listening to misplaced eloquence and unfounded rumours of violence. We're not a bunch of *women*, sir, to be frightened by your talk. I suggest we ask Lord Sarn, as Lord Lieutenant of the County, to answer Sir John Watkyn for us all. Lord Sarn, what do you say?'

And Lord Sarn is brought abruptly back from his day-dream. 'Me! Oh, taradiddle!'

With a white and angry face, Sir John Watkyn turns and stalks out of the room, leaving Anthony nonchalant as ever, Lord Sarn in another world, Marsden glowering, the trustees quite content, and Mr Pugh winking. And Rover miaows.

Along a country road, a man, dressed as a farmer, on horseback, gallops past two farmhands in a wagon. As the horseman goes off in the opposite direction he throws a crumpled piece of paper into the back of the wagon. One of the farmhands eagerly scrambles to pick it up and open it. The heads of the farmhands come together over the paper. They whisper, muted but urgent: 'Rebecca!'

In a country lane, a man is cutting the hedges. A horseman trots past him. A crumpled piece of paper falls down from the horseman near the hedger. The hedger picks it up, opens it. Again the whisper, muted but urgent: 'Rebecca!'

In an outhouse, a man is sawing wood. A figure passes quickly by the open window. A crumpled piece of paper falls down by the man.

'Rebecca!'

A cowhouse. In the morning light, we see the milk-pail, the udders of the cow, and the hands of the milker. A crumpled piece of paper is thrown to fall on the milk in the pail. The milker's hand retrieves the paper, opens it. Sound of horses' hooves galloping away. A whisper:

'The daughters of Rebecca!'

A country inn. We see a barrel of beer and the hands of a man drawing a pint mug. The hands put the full mug through the little window of a bar, then move away. On the little bar is left a crumpled piece of paper beside the pint. The first pair of hands picks up the paper and opens it. A whisper:

'They shall possess the gate.'

A sheepdog running in a field. A hand extracts a paper from under the dog's collar. A whisper:

'The gate of them that hate them.'

The farmers are moving to their secret meeting-place. On horseback they come out of their farmyards into country lanes, their lit lanterns swinging.

They ride, in small parties, into deep dark woods, a wild wind blowing.

Alone, they ride between black hedges, their lantern-lights flickering.

Out of the deep dark woods and into open country they ride together through wild wind.

Over street cobbles they come, their horses' hooves covered with sacking.

One rider, on an ancient horse, rides between tall trees, his lantern casting shadows, his umbrella swinging.

Some farmers on foot scramble down hillsides, silent and nimble as goats.

Through hedges and ditches come the young farm labourers on foot, silent and swift.

Over the fields, on a fine black horse a man rides fast, stops, tethers his horse on a tree at the dark fringe of a wood, slips through the wood and is lost.

Horsemen and men on foot, singly and in parties, swiftly, slowly, but always silently, move lanterned through the night.

And by their lantern light we see that some wear improvised black masks.

The faces of some are almost hidden under black shawls.

And most of them have blackened their faces all over.

And all of them wear skirts.

Some wear their skirts tucked well up above breeches and heavy boots, and wear above them men's dark coats and cloaks.

Others wear their skirts full length.

And some are entirely dressed as women, up to their blackened faces and shawled heads.

And a few have, from somewhere, found old curly white wigs to wear. Black faces and white wigs jog in lantern-light as the horsemen ride on.

And many of them carry shot-guns; and some have axes, some spades or pitchforks; and cattle-horns are slung from their shoulders.

We see them on the stormy skyline. All-Halloween riders, and the pitchforks they carry over their shoulders look like the horns and antlers of their familiars.

Now there is moonlight.

And now, silently, they converge from wood, lane, and field, hillside, thicket, ditch and dingle, on the far end of a disused quarry.

They all halt.

And beyond them, below the moonlit quarry fence, a man leaps up on to a great boulder and faces them.

He is black-masked.

He is disguised in traditional Welsh woman's costume, in wide black skirts and shawls. And he wears the tall, black, steeple hat.

Across his shoulder's slung a cow-horn.

The man speaks, and his voice is the voice of Anthony, disguised, though not grotesquely.

'I am Rebecca. Listen to me, my daughters, my beautiful·black-faced daughters, my bearded ladies! Never ask who I am. Never tell another who *you* are. Not even your dearest friend. Never speak *his* name or *your* name aloud. There may be those tonight who would sell you to your enemies. You are Rebecca's Daughters! It is the only

name your enemies will need to fear. Your enemies are the tollgates and those who put them up and those who grow fat on them. The gates must be destroyed. But there must be no bloodshed. If the pikemen show fight, tie them up and gag them. Do not hurt them. If you have to knock them down before you tie them up, then do it very gently. If you *have* to hurt them, let it be painless. We begin *now*! You know the first gate to destroy. You remember your instructions. Silent then, until you reach the gate. I shall be there with you.'

He leaps from the boulder into darkness.

And the crowd surges into action and begins to move away. Three men on horseback move towards the front of the crowd.

One is Mordecai Thomas, a black shawl concealing most of his face. He carries his old shabby umbrella like a raised sword.

One is Rhodri Huws, with blackened face and bare head.

The other is a farmer, whom we have seen before at Pembroke Market. He speaks excitedly. 'Darro, man, there's a fandango! Rebecca's daughters! There's a boy bach for you! Who was he? Did you know him? Where'd he come from?'

'He's the man for us,' says Rhodri. 'That's all *I* know.'

'A deliverer like unto Ehud and Gideon and Samson' begins Mordecai, but Rhodri puts a hand across his mouth. 'Hush! you fool!'

The farmer looks heavenward in joyful supplication. 'Oh let there be bang bang tonight and blood all over the shop!'

Rhodri calms him too. 'There'll be no bloodshed, didn't you hear? And don't *you* quote scriptures either. You never know who'll hear you. If you feel a quotation coming on you whistle instead!'

And he rides on, followed by the two others.

※　※　※

We see the road, the gate, and the cottage, quiet and lonely in the moonlight.

And then Rebecca's daughters appear, dismounted, with 'Rebecca' himself at the head.

Silently they advance, led by Anthony in his steeple-hat. But, as they near the tollhouse, suddenly they raise their shotguns and fire into the air, blow on their cowhorns, catcall, whistle and yell. Their lanterns bob and sway.

In the small bedroom of the tollhouse, moonlight slants across the bed in which Jack Wet, the pikeman, and his wife lie asleep.

Quickly they jump awake, sit, night-capped and astounded in bed, as pandemonium sounds below. Jack Wet stretches a shaking hand towards the candle by the bedside.

Outside, the crowd blows, bangs, hoots, howls, hullaballoos.

Anthony, at their head, raises his hand.

At once they are silent. A solitary cowhorn dies on a mooing note.

Anthony steps up to the tollhouse, stands beneath the new lighted window.

And he calls out clearly. 'Jack Wet!'

Now the candle is lit.

Jack Wet and his wife listen horrified.

Anthony's voice calls: 'Up you get!'

Jack's wife tells him timidly. 'They want you to get up.'

'I don't want to get up.'

Again Anthony's voice from outside. 'Come out, Jack Wet, and let's see you!'

'They want to see you.'

'I don't want to see *them*!'

But he gets up, in his long nightgown, goes to the window, opens a chink of curtain and looks out.

Through the chink he can see the crowd outside, wigged, bonneted, bloused and skirted, all staring up.

'Ooh!' says Jack, 'It's women!'

And suddenly from outside comes a very masculine, bass roar of voices. His wife comments timidly. 'Deep voices they got for women.'

As if to prove her point, Anthony calls again. 'Come out, and you won't be hurt. Stay where you are, and we'll burn the house down.'

Jack Wet gropes under the bed, brings out his boots, begins to put them on. He looks at his wife without affection.

'Get up. They want to see you too. I don't know why.'

'No, no, I can't. I can't go out there. I'll *freeze*!'

'Stay here and you'll cook.'

Terrified, she slides one fat leg out of bed.

The crowd surges round the tollhouse as the door opens and Jack Wet and his wife come out. They have their boots on and have flung blankets over their nightgowns, but still wear their nightcaps.

The crowd takes hold of them without violence.

'Let them see the good work!' shouts Anthony. 'Go to it, Rebecca's Daughters!'

And he turns to the direction of destruction. He gestures one section of the crowd to one end of the gate, another to the other. And these men, the strongest and wildest in appearance, lift the gate bodily from its hinges and carry it off in the direction of the river.

Now the carriers of the gate come down the riverbank, followed by many of the crowd. At a word of command from Anthony, they heave the gate into the river, eagerly helped by all the 'daughters' around them.

One of the 'daughters', Mordecai Thomas with his umbrella, watches the gate strike the water, raises his hand in a kind of benediction and opens his mouth as though to speak some apt scriptural quotation. Then, remembering, he stops, and purses his lips in a whistle instead. He whistles the first bars of a hymn tune.

Now we see, from the top of the riverbank, where Anthony stands near Jack Wet and his wife, the gate floating away down the dark river. One of the 'daughters' whispers to Jack Wet, longingly. 'If orders wasn't orders, you'd be sittin' on that gate, the both of you!'

The current bears the gate away swiftly down river. A single note is blown on a horn. And the 'daughters' who have launched the gate, and their assistants, make their way up the bank again. The gate disappears down the darkness of the river. And the horn is heard again, this time from further away.

In the morning-room of Sarn House, Lord Sarn and Sir Henry Price-Parry, cat on lap, are seated at a small table. Anthony stands near the fire, Captain Marsden a little way from him.

And in front of the table stands Jack Wet, tall hat in hand, looking as though he has been painfully scrubbed clean, stiff and awkward.

Lord Sarn looks him over. 'So you are the turnpike keeper who lost his gate the night before last?'

'Yes, my lord, but I didn't lose it, I . . .'

'You should be more careful,' Lord Sarn tells him reprovingly. 'What is your name?'

'They call me Jack Wet, sir, but my proper name is Jack Griffiths, sir. They only call me Wet for spite.'

Sir Henry, meanwhile, has poured a measure of sherry from the decanter on the table into a saucer and puts it on the floor for his cat who now laps it with pleasure. Lord Sarn beams approvingly and turns back to Wet.

'Can you describe the ringleader in this hurly-burly, Mr Wet? Was he tall, short, slim, square, oval?'

'On the tall side, sir, but you couldn't tell young or old. They all got black faces – that's cheatin'. And skirts and petticoats and ikkle bonnets and . . .'

'Yes, yes, we know all that . . . Did you recognise his voice? Or anyone else's?'

'No, sir, there was such a caterwaulin' and blowin' of cow-'orns . . . But it was the same man did all the speechin' – both times.'

Sir Henry looks up from his cat. '*Both* times?'

Jack Wet turns to him in surprise. 'Didn't you know, Sir Henry?'

'I know the Trust put up a new gate yesterday morning.'

'Yes, sir. And last night they come and take it down again.'

Sir Henry turns sharply to Marsden. '*Last* night, Captain Marsden. Did *you* know that?'

'Not a word, sir, till now.'

'It's becoming a 'abit' observes Jack Wet, gloomily.

Sir Henry is still pursuing Marsden. 'You said your men were posted on the roads last night. Were they sober?'

'I ask you to remember, Sir Henry, that I have only one troop under my command. Naturally, I did not post them at a gate that had already been attacked. And they were as sober as you are, sir.'

Lord Sarn's voice breaks in mildly. 'But what was the military doing in this affair at all? That's what *I* can't understand.'

'I acted, sir, upon an appeal for protection made to me by the Turnpike Trust.'

'Nobody told *me*.'

'My lord, I told you during dinner.'

'Are you sure I was there?'

'Certainly, m'lord. You approved of the plan.'

'What was there for dinner?'

'Jugged hare, m'lord.'

'Ah! I always agree after jugged hare. If it had been shellfish, now! Back you go to your gate, Mr Wet. I hope you find it still there.'

Jack Wet goes out and Lord Sarn proceeds with judicial gravity to shuffle the papers on the table before him. 'Let us now proceed to examine the lack of evidence . . .'

🥀　　🥀　　🥀

Down the curved stairway of Sarn House comes Rhiannon, carrying a basket. She has reached the foot of the stairs when the morning-room door opens and Captain Marsden comes out. He stops still, looks at Rhiannon. From the morning-room we hear Lord Sarn's voice ask: 'Sherry, Sir Henry?' And Sir Henry answers: 'Thankee', and the clinking of glass against decanter. The Captain closes the morning-room door and crosses to Rhiannon, who has stopped at the stair-foot. She looks up at him brightly.

'And so Rebecca's Daughters were riding again last night?'

'How did you know?'

'I listened at the door.'

Marsden is shocked and stiffly disapproving.

'Oh, don't be so haughty and dignified! Haven't you ever listened at a keyhole? Or can't you bend?'

Marsden suddenly becomes awkward and embarrassed.

'Miss Rhiannon, I wish— I wish I could understand your attitude towards me. Sometimes, you appear to like my company. . .'

'I find it very *improving*. It's like being alone with a good solid book, in a handsome, stiff binding—when you know you haven't got to read it.'

'And then sometimes, as at this moment, you appear to take pleasure in ridiculing me.'

Stiff, handsome, and awkward, he looks at her with beseeching eyes.

'You would like me to be more consistent, Captain Marsden?'

'Oh, I would!'

'And I would like you to be less. I would like to see

you dashing and gay sometimes, or wild and reckless and silly – or rakish and licentious if you like.'

Marsden, deeply shocked, can only exclaim: 'Miss Rhiannon!'

'Or anything in the world, but not always just – nobly doggy.'

Now he is deeply hurt. 'Oh, Miss Rhiannon!'

'Or doggily noble – I don't know which it is.'

He looks at her with a most sad, doggish expression. For a moment Rhiannon is contrite, but then his appearance is too much for her.

'I'm sorry if I hurt you. There, you can lick my hand.'

She puts her hand out, but scarlet-faced, haughty, and ram-rod stiff, Marsden strides down the hall and the front door slams behind him. From behind Rhiannon, Anthony's voice says: 'And he left his hat and sword behind.'

Rhiannon turns quickly, angrily. 'Were you eaves-dropping? Of all despicable habits, that's the one I hate most.'

'Unfortunately, I missed every word. I should have enjoyed it so much more than listening to arguments about the identity of Rebecca.'

'I am going into the garden now', Rhiannon tells him primly. 'You can come with me, if you want to, and watch me prune the roses. Oh I promise not to cut my finger. I know you couldn't bear the sight of blood.'

🜚    🜚    🜚

Rhiannon is pruning a rose-bush, Anthony watching her quietly and gravely. Rhiannon speaks to Anthony without looking at him.

'But who *is* Rebecca?'

'Rebecca? Oh, I had forgotten the fellow for a moment. I was writing a poem in my head, all about you and gardens and roses and singing birds and trying to think of a rhyme for Rhiannon . . . In a garden in the South . . .'

Without looking round from her pruning, Rhiannon corrects him. 'This is the West.'

'In a garden in the South, lies my lady Rhiannon . . .'

'I'm not lying, I'm standing. And I'm not your lady.'

'In a garden in the South, lies my lady *Rhiannon,* with her rose-red mouth . . .' He hesitates for a rhyme, then goes on – 'Like the mouth of a – a cannon. That doesn't fit very well, does it?'

All Rhiannon's attention is focused on the rose-bush. She ignores his poem and says primly, 'You haven't answered my question.'

'Oh, *Rebecca* again. Well, your friend Captain Marsden thinks that Rebecca is Mordecai Thomas the preacher. Sir Henry is all for Rhodri Huws. And Lord Sarn suspects himself, while sleepwalking.'

'And who do *you* think Rebecca is?'

'I think he is some small farmer, some melodramatic clodhopper, with a grievance and a taste for playing Robin Hood.'

Now Rhiannon turns for the first time to face Anthony. 'That is what you would think. I wish now that you *had* heard all the things I said to Captain Marsden.' And she looks at him straight, and talks to him with controlled, serious passion. 'I told him what kind of man it was that I could really care for. The kind of man that neither of you could ever be. Somebody who could be strong and free, and full of love and hate, who'd fight for what he believed in and stand up for people who couldn't fight for themselves. Somebody like Rebecca! Not a stiff pompous, self-righteous impossible creature who . . .'

'An excellent description of the gallant Captain!'

'And not a milksop either, who mustn't ever get his feet wet, or dirty his hands – like a fish in a muffler. And daring, *daring* to talk about a *real* man like Rebecca!'

She returns to her pruning in a fine passion. Anthony looks at her calmly, quizzically. 'I like the way your nostrils twitch when you call me "milksop". I like the way your mouth curls at the corners when you call me "a fish in a muffler". In fact, I like, *very* much, the way you look whenever you speak at all.'

And, with a little, affectionate smile, he turns from her and goes, leaving her looking after him.

By the gate outside Jack Wet's tollhouse, two dragoons stand at their horses' heads.

'Queer job, this,' says the first. 'Wish I was in bed.'

There is a pause. The horses stamp their feet.

'Wish I was drinking,' says the second. And after a pause. 'Wish I was drunk in bed.'

They look around them, beat their hands together against the cold. A long pause. An owl cries.

'Never thought when I joined the militia, I'd be up half the night waiting for a lot of men dressed up like women.'

'Wish they *was* women.'

'Then we wouldn't have the job. Sergeant'd be here.'

Suddenly there is a light in the sky, a good way off. And the two dragoons see it. After a moment it flares up brightly.

'That's them. Over at Langower. Come on!'

He shouts up to the upper window of the tollhouse. 'Hey! Jack! Jack Wet!'

A light appears in the upper window. Jack Wet comes to the window, opens it. The dragoons mount their horses. One calls up to Jack. 'You can sleep sound tonight, Jack. They're burning a gate down the road.'

'That'll be a change,' says Jack and pulls his head in, closes the window, draws the curtain.

☙ ☙ ☙

A bonfire is burning in an open clearing in the woods. No one is in sight. After a moment, the two dragoons come galloping into the clearing. They halt by the bonfire, looking about them uncertainly, then curse to themselves, realising they have been hoaxed.

Back at the tollhouse, Jack Wet and his wife are in bed. They are awakened by the sound of Anthony's voice calling: 'Jack Wet! Up you get!'

Jack turns over in bed resignedly. ''Ere they are again.' He lights a candle at the bedside. His wife rubs her eyes and grumbles. 'Why can't they take the old gate away without making us watch them? Oh, where's me boots . . .'

Jack Wet pokes his legs out of the bed clothes. His

boots are on a nearby chair. 'You should learn to keep 'em handy, like I do.'

And, sighing, they both begin to get out of bed.

☙ ☙ ☙

Through the window of a country inn, Sir John Watkyn can be seen addressing a group of men. His horse stands tethered outside. Sir John Watkyn sits at a plain wooden table. Opposite him sit Rhodri Huws, William Evan, Dave Button and Mordecai Thomas. Sir John finishes speaking with a sigh. 'So there it is. I've taken up your cause in the House of Commons, done my best to obtain sympathy for it, but the Government is averse from intervening in matters which have a purely local significance.'

Rhodri Huws looks at him with scarce concealed contempt. 'You'd have done better to speak to our Daisy. She do give milk.'

Sir John ignores this and warns seriously: 'I have to tell you – the police are coming from London.'

Rhodri grunts. 'London peelers! We'll make a batch of Welshcakes out of them.'

The landlord puts down a tray of beer mugs on the table. 'Boil 'em up for broth'd be better,' he says.

Mordecai Thomas is staring in front of him like a man possessed. 'And so Rebecca's Daughters must fight alone!'

'They cannot take the law into their own hands,' warns Sir John.

66

Dave Button laughs into his beer. 'Ask the pikemen if they can't!'

And William Evans giggles: 'Ask Jack Wet standing in the cold in his nighty.'

Sir John looks up at them sharply. 'I hope, for your own sakes, none of you here belongs to that – rabble.'

His gaze travels past William Evan, Dave Button, Rhodri Huws – all non-committal – and comes to Mordecai Thomas, who rises, like an Old Testament prophet. 'I belong to the company. And I glory in it. I preach the word of God, which is love. I respect the laws of men when they are founded upon the laws of God; but I will not bow down before them when they are founded upon the laws of evil. The evil Rebecca fights against is the evil of selfish gain, and the tyranny of rich over poor. And I will fight with Rebecca and with all who believe in what she believes, for so long as this evil remains and there is love in my heart and strength in my body.'

'Glory be' adds William Evan, reverently.

Sir John looks down his nose. 'You are a misguided man, Mordecai Thomas.'

'Thank God, I am!'

'Who is this person they call Rebecca?'

The old preacher draws himself up. 'I do not know. But *if* I knew, you could break my bones before I would tell.'

Now, we see William Evan, Dave Button and Rhodri Huws lift up their beermugs. They frame with their lips, silently, the name 'Rebecca'. And they drink.

The drawing-room at Pentre House is decorated for Christmas, and lit by candlelight. Lord Sarn with a brandy glass sits near the fire. Anthony is curled comfortably up on a chair near him, watching Rhiannon, who is at the piano, playing and singing softly. Anthony hums lightly to himself. Lord Sarn takes his nose out of the brandy glass and asks: 'What's that, my boy?'

'I was thinking how good it was to listen to music by candlelight on a winter's night, with the wind blowing outside . . .'

'All singing sounds the same to me.'

'Not Miss Rhiannon's surely, sir?'

'Oh, Rhiannon, I'm sure, is a nightingale, as singers go.'

Sara Jane comes in with coffee and tantalus, puts them down at a side table and starts to pour out. Anthony asks her: 'Is it snowing again, Sara Jane?'

'It hasn't made its mind up yet, sir.'

She starts to pass the coffee round.

'If it decides to have a blizzard,' grumbles Lord Sarn at the fireside, 'it won't stop that fellow Rebecca. Drat him!'

Anthony gives a mock shiver. 'Brrr-r! Poor Rebecca!'

Rhiannon strikes a chord and says: 'He can do without your pity, thank you. He'd *rather* be riding through *hurricanes,* at the head of his men . . .'

'His daughters, please!'

'. . . than curled up in front of the fire, smirking.'

'This isn't a smirk,' says Anthony with quiet dignity. 'It is my natural expression.'

'That is what I mean.'

As Sara Jane hands Anthony his coffee, she bends

over to whisper close in his ear. 'You're going too far, Mister Anthony, indeed you are! Always pretending like that to Miss Rhiannon. One day she's sure to find out and then . . .'

Anthony grins up at her, teasingly. She moves away. Lord Sarn yawns, hugely, and says: 'Well, thank heaven the police will be here soon.'

Rhiannon stops playing suddenly. 'The police?'

'Yes,' says her father, 'from London. Then there'll be no more trouble with Rebecca.'

'You think the police can stop him? Nobody can. He's torn down twenty gates already.'

'Mayn't they only serve to put him more on his guard, sir?' suggest Anthony.

'Ha! That's where you're wrong. They'll be in disguise, d'you see? Dressed up as labourers looking for work. Neat, eh?'

'Highly original. Whoever would have thought of it!'

Lord Sarn chuckles to himself delightedly. 'As a matter of fact, I did.'

Rhiannon strikes an angry chord on the piano and continues playing. Anthony smiles softly to himself.

☻    ☻    ☻

Two police officers, dressed roughly as casual labourers, walk together down the street towards a swinging inn sign, which says 'PENTRE ARMS'. They stop opposite the inn, and the elder cautions his companion:

Now be careful what you say. The Welsh are a sly lot. You never know what they're thinking. You keep your ears open. Don't talk more than you've got to. Just look stupid like me. Like I'm going to pretend to look, that is.'

'Yes, Inspector.'

'And don't call me Inspector! .Call me George. What's your name?'

'Walter, Inspector . . . I mean, George.'

'If I knew whose half-witted idea this was . . . Come on!'

And they cross the road to the inn.

The bar-room is quite crowded, with small farmers and farm labourers. We recognise some of them, including old William Evans and Shoni Fawr. There are games of dominoes going on.

The two police officers come in. There is sudden silence. Everyone looks at them. The domino players stop and stare. The landlord leaves a game of dominoes and comes up to them.

'Cwrw?' he asks.

The Inspector puts on his affable face. 'Good evening to *you*. Cold wind.'

'Cwrw you want?' asks the landlord again and the young policeman says: 'No! Beer!'

'Same thing,' the landlord informs him and starts to draw the beer. The police officers look about them. But nobody looks at them. The Inspector speaks to the bar in general. 'Cold weather on foot. We tramped from Templeton today.'

Nobody answers him.

'Cold in here, too,' says his companion.

The landlord brings them two mugs of beer. They

take it and as the Inspector pays, he tries to make conversation again. 'More snow coming, I think.'

'No!' says the landlord.

'Well, it's just my opinion of course . . . Will you have a pint of beer? Keep out the cold.'

'Never touch beer,' says the landlord and raises a full quart to his lips. After a moment the Inspector turns to Shoni Fawr, who is standing near. 'Will you?'

'Thought you was on the road.'

'So we are. Looking for work.'

'Then how can you afford to buy drinks for strangers? *I* can't, and *I'm* working.'

Shoni turns his back. And now William Evan joins in for the first time.

'Say you come from Templeton? Mayhap you stopped at the Black Lion?'

The young policeman is eager to please. 'Aye, we did, too. Didn't we George?'

William Evan is immediately interested. 'See my brother there? Little tiny man behind the counter with red hair and a corgi dog . . .'

The young policeman is all smiles. 'Aye, that's him. He stood us a pint.'

'Did he now? And very generous, too, seeing he's been dead these twelve years.'

The men in the bar can restrain themselves no longer, but all burst into laughter. As the laughter slowly dies, a labourer turns to Shoni Fawr and hands him a broadsheet. 'Seen this new ballad, Shoni Fawr? Handing it round in Pembroke they were, this morning.'

'What's it say, Shoni? *You* can read.'

'No spies here, boy. Speak it out aloud.'

And Shoni Fawr reads the beginning of the broadsheet ballad, chanting as he reads, while the two police officers look round at all the grinning faces in the bar.

'It was on the wild winter nights
    Of the year eighteen forty three
When the Daughters of Rebecca
    Rode out against the enemy.

'Rebecca bold was at their head
    He cared not for soldier or squire
And his Daughters in dresses and bonnets
    Were the wonder of all Pembrokeshire.

'They set out on foot and on horseback,
    Black as soot, from village and town,
To spite the proud tyrants and landlords
    And pull the tollgates down.'

The two police officers, not looking at each other, make their way out between the now silent listeners as the ballard goes on.

And their recriminations accompany them down the street . . .

'You and his brother with the red hair!'

'Well how could I know he was dead?'

'Taking a pint off a ghost!'

'I'm sorry, George.'

'And don't call me George. Call me Inspector! Now there is one man might help us. I've been hearing things about him.'

'Is he in it?'

'They're *all* in it. Now this chap I heard of, he'd sell his mother.'

'But . . .'

'I know, I know, we don't want his mother.'

They walk on in silence.

Idris Evans is working at the forge. His eyes are intent upon his work as he speaks. He doesn't look up at the Inspector, who is standing at his elbow, talking to him. Idris protests: 'I'm not the big mouth round here. I don't know nothing. I got work to do.'

'Not so much work as you used to have. Not since the trouble last year. Somebody told the magistrates, remember?'

'It wasn't me who told.'

'Some of your friends think it was, don't they?'

'I got no friends.'

'No, not now . . .'

'I'm not a man who wants friends. I go my own way.'

'So I've heard tell. You're not like the run of them round here, are you? You're different. I don't know why you stay here, in a hell of a place like this.'

'I don't want to stay here. They look at me. But where else can I go?'

'Now you listen to me, and I might be able to help you. If you were me, wouldn't you try to catch this Rebecca at one of his meetings when he tells 'em what gates he's going after? Wouldn't you?'

'He's got men on the hills, watching. By the time you got there, every man'd be gone.'

The Inspector comes closer. 'But suppose some clever fellow I'm thinking of were dressed up as one of them. He'd hear what they were up to, wouldn't he? And what time of night. And then he'd slip away, in the dark and let me know, wouldn't *you*?'

'No,' says Idris loudly. But his eyes are trapped. His 'No' is almost desperate and broken. 'What about if they caught me?'

'Catch *you*? Those fools? Besides, we'd look after you – wouldn't we? There's always jobs waiting for men like you – in better places than this.'

'I don't want to do it! I don't want to do anything bad. It's people always making me. I won't do it! I won't do it!' And tears of misery, self-pity and self-loathing are in his eyes. But later that night he sits in the little room behind the smithy, blackening his face with the aid of candle and burnt cork.

🌑    🌑    🌑

Much later still, in a disused quarry, the masked 'Rebecca' is addressing his followers: 'Daughters of Rebecca!' he cries. 'They have sent the police from London to watch us. There may be spies and informers among us – here, tonight!'

There is an angry murmur from the Daughters.

'Those of you who keep watch, see that no one slips by you, even though he is dressed as one of us! Daughters of Rebecca! We have been *too gentle*. From tonight onwards, every gate must be utterly destroyed. And not the gates alone. Destroy also the tollhouses so that not a stone remains . . .'

Axes, pick-axes, crowbars are brandished and the crowd breaks up. Among the 'daughters' is one who looks suspiciously like Idris Evans.

☙ ☙ ☙

This is the picture of the nights that follow . . .

Axes furiously descending on gates. Saws at work on gateposts. Gates blazing on fires. Fragments of gates strewing the road. Torn shreds of gates hanging from their hinges. Terrified pikemen scuttling out of doors in their nightclothes. Furniture being carried out of houses. Slates and masonry descending in clouds of dust. Houses on fire, piles of sawn up gates with notices nailed on offering 'FREE FIREWOOD'. Disguised figures hurrying on horseback by fires and falling roofs. Gagged and pinioned pikemen and their wives. A pikeman's little children clapping their hands with delight as a gate makes a great bonfire. A bound pikeman sitting on rubble under the shadow of a grandfather clock. Police officers furiously arguing – or bewildered. Idris Evans furtively and futilely making excuses for himself.

And this is the sound of the nights that follow . . . Anthony's voice calling:

> 'Jack Wet, up you get!
> Tom Brown, you come down!
> Shacki Rees, if you please!
> Dewi Pugh, it's happened to you!'

And Shoni Fawr's voice reciting from the broadsheet ballard:

'And they cried for you, all the poor of the land,
　Who were tied to the tyrant's yoke,
When Rebecca's Daughters came down on the gates
　And the tollhouses *went up in smoke*!'

At the Pentre Arms, two small farmers are sitting, legs comfortably stretched out, in front of the bar room fire, with pipes and tankards. One is reading aloud, slowly, from a local newspaper, while his companion comments.

' "Eighty gates in this county alone have been utterly destroyed".'

'It'll be eighty-three after tonight.'

' "And a great number of tollhouses razed to the ground. In the neighbouring counties scarce a gate is standing . . ." '

'We'll beat them yet!'

' "No-one can tell where Rebecca will strike next. Authority is powerless".'

'There's a lovely *ring* that's got to it! "authority is powerless".'

' "The destruction wrought by these ferocious scoundrels and incendiary rogues . . ." '

'Read that bit again, David Davies. Slowly!'

' ".The destruction wrought by these ferocious scoundrels . . ." '

Around their boardroom table, all the members of the Turnpike Trust are listening to a report from the police inspector, who is saying in an aggrieved voice: 'How can I cover every blasted . . .' he cuts off the word hurriedly. 'Every tollgate, on the roads if I haven't got the men? And no-one'll talk, *no-one,* gentlemen. They're all as innocent as babies, and I know that every *one* of 'em is up to his eyes in it. I'm expecting information from a private source but . . .'

'A wench?' suggests Mr Pugh, with a knowledgeable leer.

'. . . but I've got to have time.'

'And that,' says the first trustee, 'is exactly what you can't have . . .'

'Then if the police are useless,' suggests Sir Henry, 'we must have more troops. Agreed?'

He looks around him. All the trustees, with the exception of Anthony, who is, as usual, aloof and abstracted, nod their agreement. As does Captain Marsden. Sir Henry is about to carry on when Lord Sarn, whom nobody has ever taken into consideration, suddenly says: 'No! No more troops! It'll frighten the foxes.'

All the trustees, with the exception of Anthony, begin to speak at once. Lord Sarn looks vaguely, but unruffled, up at the ceiling. Mr Pugh speaks aside to Sir Henry: 'He actually means it, too!'

Sir Henry raises his hand to quell his colleagues. 'Then I suggest that as the Lord Lieutenant of the county has decided against that measure, we ask him to call upon the services of every well-disposed citizen – in defence of law and order, of course.'

He raises an eyebrow in the direction of Lord Sarn,

77

who says: 'I see no objection to that – unless I have to call upon myself. *I* am *not* well-disposed.'

'A volunteer force?' repeats the first trustee. 'An excellent idea. I suggest we begin by volunteering here in this very room. I'm willing for one.'

Captain Marsden sits at the table and prepares to take down names. He looks at the trustee next to him. 'I take it that you, sir . . . ?'

The man nods his head vigorously. 'Of course, of course.'

Marsden interrogates the other trustees, getting a nod or a hand held up in reply. At last he comes to Anthony. 'And Mr Raine?'

'Oh I think I might manage a little duty in the daytime.'

'But they only come out at night.'

'At night, sir? Oh no, quite impossible. I can't abide the dark.'

Captain Marsden comes, very purposefully, out of the offices of Turnpike Trust. In the square outside, stands a closed carriage, Dave Button on the driver's seat. Captain Marsden sees the carriage and strides by it, but halts, at the sound of Rhiannon's voice calling him from within. He goes back to the carriage and sees, inside, Rhiannon and her pretty young maid, Bessy. He bows stiffly and unsmilingly. She is at her most provocative.

'You know perfectly well you saw us. You are on your dignity again!'

'What is left of my dignity, Miss Rhiannon – after our last meeting.'

'There, now you are being proud and scornful with me. Have I done anything to deserve it?'

'Yes.'

Rhiannon turns to Bessy. 'Have I, Bessy?'

'Yes, Miss Rhiannon.'

'Oh, you *always* agree with men. Why do you like them so much?'

Bessy is confused, looks blushingly down at her neatly gloved and folded hands. 'Oh, Miss Rhiannon!'

'You know they're all stuffy, cautious, conceited creatures. Or nearly all of them.' The last words she says dreamily. Then she turns, almost petulantly, on Bessy again. 'How *can* you like them?'

'It must be the way I'm built, Miss,' says Bessy, shyly.

'Now you are being indelicate and horrid!'

'Yes, Miss. That is the way I'm built.'

Rhiannon in the carriage flounces away from Bessy and again addresses Captain Marsden who is standing outside looking both dignified and miserable at the same time. She fires one ironical question after another at him. 'Is your meeting over yet? Are you bringing the whole army down to catch Rebecca? You should bring the navy, too. They could shell him from our duckpond. And Bessy likes sailors, don't you, Bessy?'

'Yes, Miss. I like beards. I like pigtails too.'

The gallant Captain details his forces. 'We have my men, and the police, and the volunteers.'

'Who'll volunteer against Rebecca?' demands Rhiannon scornfully.

'To begin with, the trustees themselves.'

79

'Those dear old gentlemen! I thought they were too busy robbing the poor.'

'Sir Henry Price-Parry will be in charge.'

'What a pity they're not chasing mice. Then Sir Henry's cat could help him – if it didn't drink so much. And who else? Mr Pugh! He should feel quite at home, he's never attacked anything that wasn't in petticoats. And Mr Raine!'

'Mr Raine has refused to volunteer.'

'Oh, I'm so *glad* of that. Did you hear that, Bessy? He's refused. He's on Rebecca's side, at last!'

'Mr Raine has refused because of the cold,' the Captain points out with great self-satisfaction. And Rhiannon's momentary enthusiasm dies. 'I see,' she says coldly. 'Will my uncle be long? We are driving together to dinner.'

'He's coming now.'

'And Captain Marsden! At my fancy dress ball, you may have the first dance with me.' He looks at her in bewilderment, unable to understand her changes of mood. 'And afterwards you can take me out on to the terrace to look at the moon. You shall tell me what each of your medals stands for, and I shall listen. You may even talk to me about your horse . . .'

Lord Sarn approaches the carriage. The other trustees stand outside the turnpike offices, talking.

'Come on, Uncle, we're waiting!'

'Are we going anywhere?'

'We're going out to dinner!'

Her uncle looks around him at the darkening dusk. 'Are we now! I quite thought it was morning. A very dark morning, of course . . .' And he climbs into the carriage. A moment later he pokes his head out of the window, looks up at the sky and observes: 'With a moon, too.' And back pops his head.

Anthony comes out of the offices into the square, muffled up in his coats. He bows to the trustees and says: 'Good night, gentlemen.' The trustees turn their backs to him.

🜚     🜚     🜚

A hollow in the road, beneath a fence. Behind, lies thick woodland. In the hollow sit the volunteer patrol, which consists of five armed turnpike trustees. They are all in jovial mood. They make a little semi-circle, at one end of which sits Sir Henry's cat. Flasks and sandwiches are produced by all, and also a saucer by Sir Henry, who places it in front of the cat and pours out a measure from his flask. The volunteers drink.

'Confusion to Rebecca!'

'To the volunteers!'

'To the turnpike trusts!'

'To us!'

'To the ladies!' adds Mr Pugh and the cat 'Miaow!'

All settle themselves comfortably.

'What a nice quiet gate to guard!'

'Right on the main coach road.'

'The last one they'd dare attack!'

'Very well chosen indeed!'

They drink again, filled with bonhomie, spirits and security. There is a pause. 'Quite a nip in the air tonight,' observes one of their number, and 'Regular Anthony Raine-y weather!' rejoins Sir Henry.

As the laughter fades, Mr Pugh begins to speak in the voice of one who has all the time in the world on his hands and an improper story to tell. 'It reminds me of a night many years ago, when I was a proper terror! Now what was the girl's name? My, but she was frightened of me! Rosie, was it? Or Rene? No, no – Rachel! Or Ruby. Or . . .'

'I hope it wasn't Rebecca!' observes Sir Henry. And almost on the name a pair of hands is thrust through the fence and gags him. Another pair pinions his hand. And suddenly the scene is swarming with masked 'Rebecca's Daughters.' And all the terrified volunteers are disarmed, gagged and bound, and laid out against the bank.

Anthony, dressed as Rebecca, appears on horseback, on the road, surveying the scene. 'Good! Now for the gate and tollhouse.'

The clattering of a horse's hooves is heard in the distance as the men begin to break away. Anthony raises his hand. 'Wait!' And he wheels his horse round to face the approaching horseman. Mordecai Thomas, reins up by Rebecca. 'There's a coach on the road!', he whispers.

'I'll come with you,' says Anthony and calls to the 'Daughters'. 'Begin on the gate!'

He and Thomas ride off. The 'Daughters' swarm off in the other direction, leaving the trustees looking up at the stars. One solitary Rebecca-man is left who, after a furtive and hurried look around him, hurries after the rest. He is Idris Evans, the informer. The cat strolls among the bound trustees, lapping up the spirits from their spilt flasks. He rubs himself against Sir Henry's pinioned legs.

Lord Sarn's carriage, driven by Dave Button, is coming along the moonlit road. Inside it Lord Sarn is fractious, Rhiannon is impatient, and Bessy silent. Lord Sarn grumbles: 'I'll never go out to dinner again. The soup tasted of beetles.'

'You've never tasted beetles.'

'I'm older than you, aren't I? I might have been a famous beetle-taster in my youth for all you could know. Things have come to a pretty pass when a man's niece tells him to his face that he hasn't eaten beetles.'

'Oh, Uncle!' says Rhiannon, exasperated, 'I don't care if you eat all the cockroaches in the kitchen.'

Lord Sarn pounces triumphantly: 'Ha! Want to poison me now, eh?'

The coach pulls up with a jerk. Lord Sarn is thrown against Bessy who gives a little scream.

Outside, Dave Button looks down at two riders, Rebecca and Thomas, who are blocking the road. He winks. The coach window is opened and Lord Sarn looks out.

'Highwaymen!' His head pops back. 'I'd never have believed it. I thought the last highwayman was hanged twenty years ago.'

Anthony's masked face appears at the window. Lord Sarn calls loudly: 'It's no good! I've left my watch at home!'

Looking at Anthony in wonder, Rhiannon breathes: 'Rebecca!'

Lord Sarn is still protesting. 'Forgot me money. There's no gold in me teeth neither!'

Anthony disappears from the window and Dave Button comes to it. He has his hands above his head. 'It's Rebecca, sir, and one of his daughters . . .'

'Shouldn't keep his daughter out on a night like this,' Lord Sarn tells him.

'He's got a pistol in my back. He says I'm to drive on till we reach the tollgate. Then you and Miss Rhiannon and Bessy, m'lord, are to get out and see them burn the gate down, m'lord . . . I got to do what he says, m'lord.'

'Then don't be a fool! Do it!'

Dave Button, his hands still above his head, disappears from the window. The coach moves on. Rhiannon turns excitedly to Bessy: 'We're going to see them! Rebecca and his Daughters! Oh, Bessy, perhaps I can *talk* to him!'

'How many men will there be, do you think?'

'Oh, lots and lots of them! And they're all daring and fierce with torches and hatchets and everything and all of them with wild black faces and . . .'

Lord Sarn's voice breaks in. 'A pleasant evening, I must say. First beetles in the soup and then black men with hatchets!'

Up on the box, Dave Button is grinning with delight, singing a little song to himself, and conducting himself with his whip.

> 'It was on a wild winter's night
>    Of the year eighteen forty three
> When the Daughters of Rebecca
>    Rode out against the enemy . . .'

The coach drives up to the tollgate, which is now in the process of being destroyed. Anthony and Mordecai Thomas ride just behind the coach, one on either side. The coach stops. Anthony waves his pistol at Dave Button who climbs down and opens the coach door. And Rhiannon, followed by Bessy and Lord Sarn come out. There is the noise of sawing and hacking. At a gesture of command from Anthony, some masked and face-blackened Rebecca-ites take charge, without violence, of Lord Sarn and Dave Button and lead them to a point of vantage from which they can see the destruction of the gate in detail. Lord Sarn is cool as ever. 'If I must watch this entertainment, I demand a chair to sit on,' he says.

One of his captors waves a hand to the Rebecca-ites, who are bringing the furniture out of the tollhouse. 'A chair for his lordship!' And with ironic solemnity two large 'Daughters' bring over to Lord Sarn an old, delapidated rocking chair. With dignity, Lord Sarn accepts the offering and sits.

Rhiannon and Bessy stand near the coach, watching the destruction. Anthony, disguised, on horseback, is very close to them. Rhiannon looks up earnestly at Anthony who takes no notice of her but looks sternly ahead of him. She whispers his name. 'Rebecca!'

He does not acknowledge her. She tries again. 'Rebecca! I want to tell you that I believe in you. I believe that what you're doing is right. It's the only thing left for the people to do. If no one will listen to them at all, they've got to destroy the gates.'

Bessy who is paying no attention to Rhiannon's words but is excitedly staring at the scene before her, now pulls at Rhiannon's sleeve. 'Oh Miss, there's a man over there, like a pirate!'

Rhiannon does not heed her. She speaks again to 'Rebecca'. 'Rebecca, if I was a man I'd be one of your Daughters. I think you're good, and brave.'

Still 'Rebecca' aloofly and sternly takes no notice of her. Now Bessy pulls her mistress's sleeve again. 'Miss, the one like a pirate, he's giving his lordship a rock!'

There sits Lord Sarn, in his rocking chair. And immediately behind him stands a tall, fierce-looking 'Daughter' with blackened face who, automatically, without thinking, rocks the chair with one huge hand. And Lord Sarn, as though it were the most natural thing in the world, sits, being rocked to and fro, watching the demolition of the tollhouse.

Rhiannon watches adoringly as Anthony urges his horse into the middle of the activity, raises his pistol and fires it once into the air. On one finger of his hand, as he does so, shines a large and peculiarly shaped signet-ring. The shot is the signal for torches to be applied to the broken gate and the empty and partly demolished tollhouse. In a moment, fires are blazing. Another sign from Anthony and Lord Sarn and Dave Button are being hurried to the coach. Lord Sarn is pushed into the coach, Dave Button hustles up into the driver's seat. At an imperious sign from Anthony, Rhiannon and Bessy step into the coach. A 'Daughter' closes the door. And as the coach moves away, Rhiannon puts her head out through the window and calls: 'Good night, dear Rebecca!'

Two 'Daughters' watch the coach as it drives away. One, Mordecai Thomas, is holding his horse. The other is Idris Evans.

' "Dear Rebecca". Glory be!' exclaims Mordecai. 'She is a wicked wench, like unto Aholibah and Jezebel . . .'

86

Idris Evans looks at him closely and asks: 'Mr Mordecai Thomas is it?'

Mordecai is off guard for the moment. 'Yes,' he says, 'who is that?'

He raises his mask and peers at Idris Evans, who moves silently and quickly away. Thomas stares uneasily after him.

Next morning, Mordecai Thomas, now dressed in his ordinary ministerial black, stands in Sarn Hall, before a table at which sit Lord Sarn, the two police officers, and Captain Marsden. The second police officer is taking notes, as his Inspector reads the charge. '. . . and you are arrested on information as aiding and abetting an unlawful act.'

'Who informed against me?' demands Thomas sternly.

'You are not here to ask questions.'

'It does not matter. Satan's claw is on him.'

'He won't like that,' observes Lord Sarn, urbanely. 'You will be remanded in custody until you can be charged in court. Were you *really* there, Mr Thomas?'

'Voice and features both sworn to, sir,' puts in the Inspector.

'Well, I hope you weren't the one who gave me a push in the back, right in the lumbago.'

'I was there,' admits Thomas. 'I do not deny it.'

Captain Marsden takes a hand. 'What is Rebecca's real name?'

'I do not know it.'

'Do you know the names of any of the rioters?'

'I do not.'

'There was one with a poke bonnet on,' recollects Lord Sarn. 'He let me sit down in a chair to watch the fun' – he changes the word quickly – 'the disgraceful scene. I wish I knew his name.'

'You refuse to give any information?' asks the gallant Captain.

'I inform against no one.'

Marsden turns aside angrily. 'You can lock him up, Inspector.'

'Yes sir, but where?'

'The cells at the courthouse. Where else?'

'There's only one cell, sir, and it's occupied. Two of your men, sir. Drunk as lords.' He remembers the presence of Lord Sarn. 'I beg your pardon, sir . . .'

The second policeman looks up from his notes. 'There's an old lock-up, Inspector, in his lordship's park. I saw it this morning.'

'No, no,' protests his lordship. 'I keep my gardening tools there. And the croquet hoops. And jars full of things. And butterfly nets.'

'It would be a great help to us, m'lord.'

'Oh, very well. Tell Dave Button the coachman to clear a place for him. And see that he gives Mr Thomas luncheon.'

'I will eat the bread of affliction and . . .'

Lord Sarn corrects him. 'You'll eat pigeon pie like the rest of us.'

The two police officers and Marsden rise and conduct Mordecai Thomas out of the room. They have reached the door when Lord Sarn's voice halts them. 'Are you sure you would not like something to while away the time, Mr Thomas? A musical instrument or . . .' But Thomas walks out, holding himself erect, and the police officers hurry after him.

Thomas is being taken out through the front door by the two police officers. Marsden follows a little way behind. He stops at the sound of Anthony's voice, calling 'Bravo, Captain!'

Marsden turns and sees Anthony at the foot of the stairs. 'My congratulations. It has taken only the London police, your men and yourself, the gallant volunteers, *and* an informer, to catch one harmless fanatic. When do you attack the cradles? They are full of infant Rebeccas.'

Marsden comes towards him up the hall, his hands clenched by his sides. 'One day, sir, you will go too far.'

'One day, sir you will go to the theatre in Drury Lane and see how that line is properly acted. The left foot forward, the fist upraised, the brow darkened.'

And Captain Marsden, dark-browed, with one fist raised, comes a few steps forward. Anthony applauds. 'Excellent! You would make a name for yourself on the stage. I shan't tell you *what* name . . .'

As Marsden goes nearer to Anthony, with every intention of striking him, Rhiannon comes down the stairs and asks: 'Are you rehearsing for a play?'

Marsden lets his fist fall and mutters grimly to Anthony: 'I hope it *is* a rehearsal.'

'We *both* look forward to the first performance. I think it will be a knock-out.'

Rhiannon comes between them. 'I think you're quarrelling. Why do you always do it in the hall?' She turns to Anthony. 'And why do you come here to-day? Just to sneer at my friends?'

'I came to condole with you on your unfortunate experience last night. You met Rebecca?'

'Yes. And it was not unfortunate.'

Captain Marsden turns to her with gallant anxiety. 'He didn't treat you roughly? If he did . . .'

'I don't need your protection, Captain Marsden, or your condolences, Mr Raine. Oh, you both think I've made a hero out of him, don't you? Well, I have. He *is* a hero, and you're both . . . Oh, I don't know what you are! All you can do is to arrest poor little Mr Thomas – a great big hulking man like you! And all you can do is shiver at home . . .'

Anthony completes the sentence for her. '. . . a great big hulking man like me. We are a pair, aren't we, Captain?'

'I'm disgusted with you both.'

The Captain is deeply hurt. 'Oh, Miss Rhiannon. Not me, surely!'

'Yes, you too, you old – you old – St Bernard, you!'

And indeed Captain Marsden is looking at her like a big gloomy dog.

'Oh, Miss Rhiannon!' exclaims Anthony, mocking her – and she turns on him. 'Yes, you as well, you niminy-piminy. You neither of you deserve to be invited to the masked ball. I wish Rebecca were coming to it instead . . . And now I'm going to say good morning to you. And don't you dare quarrel in the drive.'

90

Anthony and Marsden bow to Rhiannon, and go down the hall to the front door. Anthony opens it, and, with a flourish, indicates that Marsden is to go first. 'Remember, Captain,' he says, 'we are not to quarrel in the hall or the drive. Where shall we choose, next time?'

Marsden stiffly, without looking at Anthony, passes him through the open door. They walk down the drive, one on each side of it, Marsden stiff as a ramrod, Anthony whistling. He is whistling the tiny snatch of tune we heard from Dave Button earlier.

In the small drawing-room of Sarn Hall, his lordship is trying on fancy dress costumes in front of a mirror, while Rhiannon plays softly at the piano. He picks up a cocked hat and puts it on his head and looks in the mirror, trying it at different angles. 'Am I an admiral or a beadle now?'

'Neither, dear, you're a highwayman.'

Hastily Lord Sarn puts the hat down, tries on a Spanish mantilla, a Dutch girl's bonnet, a Turkish fez, one after the other. 'I've had enough of highwaymen. I want a peaceful fancy dress. Can't I go as a bishop, or a bellows-mender?'

'We haven't the costumes, uncle.'

'Or a rat-catcher, or a maharajah, or a . . .'

'No! You'll go as Henry the Eighth. You know you always go as Henry the Eighth. People expect it of you.'

'Why can't I go as a Chinese mandarin or a dairy-maid?' I haven't the figure for Henry the Eighth. Nor the wives, neither . . . Or an Indian brave, or an Amazon warrior, or a bootboy . . .'

'Henry the Eighth's is a very handsome costume and you look very handsome in it. You don't want to spoil *my* pleasure, do you?'

'No, no, of course not, my dear. I.won't say another word.' Absentmindedly he tries on another article of fancy dress before the mirror. 'Could I come as Father Christmas? It's snowing outside.'

'Oh, Uncle! If it's snowing, then Anthony Raine will come as a hearthrug . . .'

A footman comes in with a note on a salver which he brings to Rhiannon. She quickly opens it. 'Anthony Raine won't be coming at all. "I must inform you that owing to the inclemency of the weather" . . . The over-weening effeminate little minikin! I hate him.'

She crumples the note into a ball and throws it away and begins to play again; the same music, but this time very fiercely. Lord Sarn smiles a secret smile at her stiff back and says: 'I can be just as strong-minded as you, my dear. I will not go to the ball tonight as Henry the Eighth! I fancy myself as a laughing Jester, with bells on!'

☺     ☺     ☺

But that night, when the great morning-room has been cleared for the ball, Lord Sarn comes down the stairs to join the fancy-dressed, masked dancers, wearing the costume of Henry the Eighth.

And at that moment, Anthony is arriving at the front

door, disguised as 'Rebecca' in full dress, wide skirted and steeplehatted, with a black mask. The footman who opens the door to him is terrified, but his terror vanishes as Anthony flutters a formal invitation card under his nose. Smiling, the footman steps aside to let Rebecca into the hallway. As Anthony strides across the hall towards the open doors of the morning room, the band strikes up the opening bars of a Strauss waltz. He reaches the open doors and looks into the room.

The masked guests are dancing, or sitting out, or standing in groups in corners with glasses in their hands. Footmen are moving with trays among the guests. Lord Sarn is drinking with Sir Henry Price-Parry who is a very stout Dick Whittington, his cat beside him, and Mr Pugh with his pitted Punch-like nose, is dressed as a small Don Juan. Rhiannon is dancing with Captain Marsden.

Then suddenly Lord Sarn looks up and sees Anthony. He spills his drink. Sir Henry's cat laps it up. Mr Pugh and Sir Henry follow his glance. They stand dumbstruck. And suddenly the attention of all the guests is centred on the ballroom door. Surprise ripples among them. Rebecca stands in the doorway surveying the scene, his hand on his belted pistol.

Rhiannon is dancing with Captain Marsden, but her eyes are on Rebecca. 'Oh, Rebecca *has* come!' she whispers. 'He *has* come to my party. Just as I wished.'

'Nonsense, my dear Miss Rhiannon,' says the Captain superciliously. 'It is merely some mannerless young nobody with a . . .'

Rhiannon interrupts him without looking at him. She does not shift her gaze. 'And you are *somebody*? Then I wish you were somebody else! And please to keep that tone of your voice for your future wife, Captain Marsden . . .'

'Really, Miss Rhiannon, I . . .'

'Perhaps the unfortunate young woman will appreciate it. She will have little else to appreciate, goodness knows! Oh, *look* at him!'

'I have no wish to spoil the dance by . . .'

'Spoil it, sir? You dance as though you had been left out all night to freeze on the washing line . . . You *creak*, Captain Marsden.'

They dance on, Rhiannon's gaze, rapt and abstracted, Marsden's hurt and sorrowful.

Across the room, Rebecca crosses the floor, past the dancers, to a young lady sitting out. He bows and presents himself. She is charmed to accept. They dance.

Lord Sarn, Sir Henry and Mr Pugh watch Rebecca and his partner dance.

'It seems to me to be in the worst of taste,' huffs Sir Henry, but Mr Pugh protests, with a leer: 'Her partner doesn't think so. She trembles like a moth before the flame. *I* used to make them feel like that – before I burned them up!'

'Who *is* he?' asks Lord Sarn. 'Do I know him? I can't recognise anyone tonight. Wouldn't know my own brother, poor dear Silvanus – except that he always danced sideways like a crab.'

'He's making his partner blush,' reports Mr Pugh, approvingly. 'Good fellow!'

'Sideways Sarn they used to call him. Kept him locked up in the west wing for years. With his harp and his marmoset.'

On the floor, Lady Price-Parry and her partner are also discussing Rebecca.

94

'Just like the creature himself,' she says.

'But surely, *you* haven't seen him?'

'Oh, la, no! I go by my husband's description. After that night he spent tied up in a ditch.'

'A very distressing night for Sir Henry.'

'Yes, very. And it wasn't even a ditch he knew.'

The same subject occupies Rhiannon and the Captain . . . 'He dances beautifully!' she says.

'Like a dancing-master!'

'In spite of all those skirts and petticoats and things. I wonder whether he wears . . . I mean, I wonder whether he wears women's dancing shoes as well. I can't quite see.'

'Would you keep the next dance for me, Miss Rhiannon?'

'Thank you very much, Captain Marsden, but the next dance – I shall sit out.'

The music within has stopped. Bessy is walking across the hallway to the stairs and beginning to climb them when Dave Button, coming from the direction of the kitchen quarters, stops her.

'Bessy, Bessy!'

'I mustn't stop now, Mr Button, the ladies'll be coming upstairs to powder.'

'Stop a moment!'

'I mustn't.'

'I don't mean I want to kiss you, you goose!'

'Oh, I thought you did. You usually do.'

'Is it true there's one of the gentlemen dressed up like Rebecca?'

'Yes, it is, too. I thought I'd scream when I saw him.'

'I never heard *you* scream yet, Bessy bach.'

'He was so exactly like him, I nearly fainted, honest

I did, only I didn't because Mr Pugh might pick me up and then . . . You go and see for yourself. By the curtain by the door there. Nobody'll notice.'

And with a smile to him, she goes on up the stairs. Dave Button moves down the hall towards a curtain at the side of the open ballroom door. He looks through a chink in the curtain and then says to himself, in an awestruck voice: 'It's *true*! Oh, bless my bunions!'

He presses his eye closer to the curtain chink as the music of a new dance begins from within.

Rebecca, the music begun, is crossing the empty floor to where Rhiannon sits with a young masked partner. She looks up at Rebecca, a little, almost timid, smile dawning on her lips. Her partner leaves with a bow. Wordlessly, she rises and comes close to him, and they begin to dance. The rest of the dancers move on to the floor. We follow Rhiannon and Rebecca dancing. Marsden and partner come into picture, Marsden watching them jealously. But they are oblivious of him. She is looking up at her partner, still with that little smile on her lips. And he looks down, quietly and gravely, at her. We see his hand – the hand that Rhiannon, too, can see, fasten more firmly on hers. At the increase of the pressure on her hand, Rhiannon looks at his. And on one of the fingers of his hand she sees the large and peculiarly shaped signet ring. Her eyes widen. Then she looks up at him again, at the eyes behind the mask and smiles, this time not shyly nor timidly but with full certainty of love.

'I wished you to come Rebecca,' she says softly. 'With all my heart I did.'

Dave Button, shielded by the curtain is peering in at the dancers. Rhiannon and Rebecca dance by. He makes

little, furtive gestures to attract Rebecca's attention.

'And dancing with *her*!' he whispers to himself. 'Oh, Mafoozulum!'

Rhiannon speaks softly as she dances in Anthony's arms. 'You came to me! You came to me! You mustn't talk, must you? Then I would know who you really are. But I'd never tell! You can speak to me, Rebecca, for ever you can. I'd cross my heart, only you're holding my hand. You can speak to me. But not here. Dance towards the terrace doors.'

And they dance towards the doors that lead out on to the terrace. Quietly, Rebecca opens them and they pass through on to the terrace, which is sheltered from the weather. Rhiannon takes off her mask and looks at Rebecca.

'Now you can speak to me. There's no one to hear you now, only me, and I'm as quiet as . . . as quiet as . . . Oh, I don't want to say "as quiet as the grave". That sounds sad, and I'm not sad at all. Not now. Take off your mask.'

But Rebecca makes no sound or movement, only looks at her.

'Tell me who you are. You came tonight because we met on the road. Because you saw me once and you wanted to see me again. Didn't you? Didn't you? Tell me that's why you came. I knew it was you. I didn't really need to see that ring on your finger . . . Who gave you the ring? Was it somebody you love? Oh, no, it couldn't be. Because you came tonight only to see *me*. Oh, you shouldn't have come! No, no, I don't mean that, but it's *terribly* dangerous for you. But you didn't mind how dangerous it was. You didn't mind, did you? Oh, speak to me, please. I'm saying all the things that I want *you* to say to me. Take off your mask.'

Rebecca has stood through this, quite still. Now suddenly he bends down and kisses her on the mouth. For a moment she holds fast to him. Then, at the end of the kiss, he moves, swiftly, and yet gently away from her and vaults over the snow-covered balustrade and disappears.

In the park, in the snow, against a background of trees, almost merging into them, stands Dave Button waiting. In the distance, the music from the ballroom can be heard. Anthony's voice is heard, calling him.

In a loud whisper, Dave replies: 'Here I am!'

Anthony, as Rebecca, comes through the trees. Dave looks at him admiringly. 'You gave me the wobblies when I saw you frisking in there, mun.'

'You had the message?'

'Aye, but how was I to know you'd be dancing there among 'em as bold as a dragon. How'd you get in the ball? Did they send Rebecca an invite?'

'They did and they didn't. You've got the horse?'

'That's tribulation number one. There isn't no horse. I couldn't pinch one. The stable's full of the gentlemen's grooms.'

'He'll have to have mine. Now, quick!'

He leads the way across the park.

The lock-up is an old one-storied little building, with an almost flat roof and small barred windows. In one of the windows a feeble light is shining. The small clearing in which the building stands is surrounded by shrubs and trees. A constable with a shot gun comes round the corner of the lock-up. He is eating a large sandwich, and takes a perfunctory peep through the lighted window. He vanishes again round the corner. Anthony and Dave Button appear and Anthony runs lightly across to the lock-up and swings himself up on to the roof. He hangs there, in his black skirt, like a great bat.

The constable is sitting on a log outside the door of the lock-up, eating. An owl hoots. The sound does not disturb him. The owl hoots again. This time he looks up and around him in the darkness lit by the light from the barred window.

Now flat on the roof, Anthony cups his mouth and wails: 'Beware Rebecca! Beware Rebecca and her daughters!'

The constable leaps to his feet, stands open-mouthed for a moment, then moves stealthily round the corner.

Dave Button is among the trees. He deliberately shakes the branches, making a crackling noise on the still cold night air.

The constable is advancing along the side of the lock-up towards where the black bat figure of Anthony on the roof lies waiting. The branches crackle again, and the constable looks quickly in the direction of the noise, unslings his gun, and moves cautiously a few steps, until he is directly below Anthony.

Anthony swoops down from the roof on top of the constable. They struggle on the ground; then Anthony masters the constable and gags him with a handkerchief and rolls him over.

Dave Button joins them, bends down and detaches keys from the constable's belt.

'Tribulation number two,' he whispers. 'For *him*.'

'Quick – now!'

Dave Button disappears. The constable shows signs of coming to. Anthony, one hand pinioning him down face to the ground, dives among his own voluminous skirts and pulls out a length of rope and binds the man's wrists and ankles. Then he jumps to his feet and moves quickly away.

Mordecai Thomas and Dave Button waiting in shadow. Anthony joins them, takes Thomas by one arm, Dave Button by the other, and they rush him into the dark trees straight ahead. As they plunge into darkness distant cries are heard of 'Help! Help!'

The constable has got rid of his gag and wrist-ropes and is struggling to set free his ankles. He continues to shout as he frees himself. 'Help! Help! Hundreds of Rebeccas! Help!'

Anthony, Dave Button and Thomas hurrying along a wooded path, Thomas breathing heavily. Suddenly Thomas slips and falls. He writhes on the ground. 'My ankle's gone.'

'Tribulations always come in threes!' mutters Dave Button.

They try to help Thomas to his feet, manage to do so at last and half carry him along. There are cries behind them in the darkness.

Anthony tells Dave. 'You get back!'

'I stay with you.'

Thomas groans: '*Both* of you get away!'

Dave Button grabs one of his arms and says, affectionately: 'Listen to the old stupid.'

And they half carry him onwards.

Outside the lock-up now are the Inspector and a sergeant and two other constables. The freed constable is breathlessly gabbling his experience. 'They all swoop down on me, out of the air, with pistols and . . .'

The Inspector barks an order to the sergeant: 'Warn the patrol to cover every road and lane round the estate. Shoot on sight!'

The sergeant runs off. The constable is still full of his experiences. '. . . and one of 'em knocked me down with a log o' wood and two of 'em jumped on my back and pressed me nose in a nuisance and . . .'

The Inspector tells the other men: 'Go up to the stables and get those grooms out on the search!' And as they hurry away, he turns on the constable and growls: 'And you! Stop your gabbling!'

In the park, a gate, with a horse tethered. Anthony and Dave Button hoisting Thomas on to it.

'Don't go near the lodges,' Anthony tells him. 'Follow the long hedge on the sheltered side, the snow's not drifted there. Then over the next field, across the road, and you come to the drive to Pentre House; ride straight up . . .'

'To Pentre House?' asks Thomas, amazed, and Dave Button adds: 'No, no! Not there, boy bach!' But Anthony persists; 'Go round to the back door. You will be let in. I'll follow you.'

He whacks his horse across the rear. And Thomas rides off. Anthony turns to Dave. 'And you get back to Sarn Hall!'

'Yes, Mr Anthony,' says Dave softly.

And quickly the two men part in different directions into the darkness. The cries of the pursuers can be heard in the distance.

On the terrace, Rhiannon, unmasked, is looking out towards the dark park. She stands in a pool of light thrown from the ballroom, still and tranquil. But suddenly, in the distance, among trees, can be seen the will-o'-the-wisps of lanterns, far fireflies. And her tranquillity is broken. An expression of uncertainty crosses her face. And at last, she turns and opens the doors into the morning room.

Here, the guests are still dancing, Lord Sarn among them. Rhiannon comes into the room from the terrace. She is still unmasked. Captain Marsden, inattentive to his dancing partner, sees her come in. His face hardens into suspicious jealousness. As she begins to move down the side of the room, avoiding the dancers on the floor, she looks around suddenly, aware of some scrutiny, and catches Marsden's eye. His eyes are fixed on hers, compellingly. She puts up her fingers to her face, as though his gaze were burning it, and discovers that she is unmasked. She lowers her eyes, adjusts her mask and moves off down the side of the room again and is lost to sight among the dancers.

Out in the park, the figure of Rebecca dodging from one patch of cover to another round the corner of a snow-covered field, moving swiftly along under the cover of a high hedge running across a large snowy meadow. We follow the figure of Rebecca sometimes running, sometimes stopping and crouching towards a gate in a high hedge. Beyond this gate is the road. Now we see Rebecca close as he moves – sometimes, in his black dress, lost in black shadows, and sometimes caught blackly against the white of the snowed field – towards the gate. He reaches the gate and is about to climb it when he draws quickly back and crouches low. Two mounted troopers come into picture, on the road beyond the gate, their horses silent on the snow. The troopers carry carbines and sabres. One trooper moves off along the road and out of the picture. The other sits his horse motionless in the moonlight, directly opposite the gate. With infinite caution Rebecca crawls back to the shelter of the hedge and starts back in the direction he has come . . .

Now the figure of Rebecca running fast and silent in the shadow of a hedge towards another gate. He stops suddenly and listens. There is dead silence. Quickly he climbs the gate, like a black witch climbing a broom, and is in a country lane. He runs, still close to the hedge, up the lane towards a corner. Now we see him close as he prepares to round the corner. Tentatively, crouched very low in the ditch of the lane, he peers round the corner.

A mounted trooper on his black horse seen from the level of the ditch. The trooper has his carbine resting ready in his arms. Trooper and horse look enormous. Anthony draws back from the corner and runs, snow-silent, down the lane, under cover of the hedge, in the direction from which he has come. He has just reached the gate when, round the far corner of the lane bob a number of shining lanterns. He climbs the gate. For a moment his black shape is seen clearly in the moonlight. The lanterns coming from the far corner bob frenziedly. There are cries from behind and among the lanterns. And then the black figure drops over the gate and is gone.

Now, attracted by the cries, the mounted trooper rides quickly and silently round the other corner. He dismounts at the gate which Rebecca has just climbed and peers over the gate. The cries and the lanterns are nearing him.

He, too, climbs the gate and is gone. And, after him, a group of armed and lanterned men on foot clamber the gate and are lost to us.

☙ ☙ ☙

In the morning-room, all is music and dancing and gossip. Rhiannon stands alone near a window. The curtains across the window are only partially drawn. With a troubled expression, Rhiannon is looking out of the window into the night.

Sir Henry Price-Parry and Mr Pugh are standing with glasses in their hands. On a chair near them, the figure of Sir Henry's cat is stretched out flat on its back. Mr Pugh is looking slyly round the room. 'Miss Rhiannon's come back from the terrace,' he says.

'I didn't know she'd gone,' says Sir Henry, without interest. Mr Pugh catches sight of the cat. 'What's the matter with Rover?'

Sir Henry looks at his pet and says briefly: 'Mixed his drinks.'

Mr Pugh again leerily and blearily spies round the room. 'But the young man dressed as Rebecca, he hasn't come back.' With relish, 'Ho! I suspect the worst.'

Lady Price-Parry and another lady are sitting out watching the dancing.

'Poor, dear Rhiannon isn't dancing. I don't think her heart is in it tonight.'

'Perhaps she left it out on the terrace. And of course, there *is* a moon.'

'Ah, the number of times I have lost my heart on a moonlit terrace.'

'And,' observes Lady Price-Parry, in a honeyed voice, 'the number of times it has been found and returned to you, my dear.'

Captain Marsden is dancing inattentively with a very pretty, very young partner. He is looking anxiously over her shoulder as they dance. She is talking ... '. . . and I don't think you've heard a word I've been saying and I think you're very rude and I'll never dance with you again and you trod on my toe, like a nelefant and you never said . . .'

Marsden breaks in, anxiously. 'Please do excuse me!'

'Well, that's better!'

'Thank you so much!'

And he breaks away from her and makes his way through the other dancers, leaving her indignantly speechless.

Marsden moves across the floor to Rhiannon at the window. Her face is pale as she looks through the partially-curtained window into the night. He tells her agitatedly: 'You're looking unwell. Shall I bring you something? Sal volatile? A glass of water?'

Rhiannon does not look at him, but answers faintly: 'Yes, please!'

As he hurries off, she continues to look through the half curtained window at the dark groups of figures carrying lights, as they run across the park towards the further trees, and disappear into them. Then the park outside the house is empty.

Marsden meanwhile hurries up to Sir Henry and Mr Pugh. 'A glass of water please. Quickly!' Mr Pugh hands him a glass full of a colourless liquid.

Marsden hurries back to Rhiannon, presses it into her hand. And, without thinking and still staring out, she drinks. One gulp, and she splutters and coughs.

Mr Pugh and Sir Henry. Mr Pugh is looking with pleasure in Rhiannon's direction. He sniggers: 'It wasn't water. That was creme-de-menthe . . .'

Rhiannon, gasping after her drink, the tears running down her face, her glass still in her hand, Marsden solicitiously standing near.

Suddenly, looking through tears across the room, she makes an agitated gesture. A footman is standing in the doorway, anxiously glancing among the dancers. He sees Lord Sarn dancing and, moving unceremoniously through the guests, reaches him. Lord Sarn and his partner stop dancing. The footman whispers. Lord Sarn takes off his mask and forces his way towards the orchestra. He gestures them to silence. The music peters out. Lord Sarn addresses the guests, all of whom are now standing still, whispering among themselves and watching him. 'Ladies and gentlemen, please keep perfectly calm. There is nothing for anyone to be alarmed about. A tollgate rioter imprisoned in these grounds has been forcibly released by armed men of an unknown number headed by the desperado Rebecca himself. The man Rebecca, I now suspect, was dancing here in this room tonight. Let us hope this house is not burned over our heads and that there will not be overmuch bloodshed in the ballroom. I repeat: There is nothing for anyone to be alarmed about.'

An elderly lady screams. Lord Sarn continues: 'Rebecca and his men are liable, as gaol-breakers, to be shot on sight . . .'

A shot is heard outside, not far off. The glass drops from Rhiannon's hand, shatters on the floor. Marsden looks at her sharply, jealously. Lord Sarn, imperturbable, concludes; '. . . But everything will be all right in the end, I assure you – if we live to see it.'

Consternation among the ladies. Captain Marsden hurries towards the door and addresses the guests, most of whom have now pulled off their masks. 'Ladies and gentlemen, please remain where you are.' And he hurries out.

Out in the park, from a belt of trees beyond the snow-covered lawn, the figure of Rebecca comes running and, looking in every direction, rests for a moment by a tree. The light of a lantern flashing not far off warns him, and he breaks cover, running over the lawn towards the house. He reaches the house where the windows are not lighted and begins to climb the ivy.

Two grooms appear against the background of trees. One suddenly and excitedly points up at the black figure of Rebecca high up against the ivy of the house.

'Look mun!'

'Like a witch!' says the other. They run off.

Back in the morning-room, a hubbub of unmasked guests. Lord Sarn is quickly drinking. Rhiannon stands pale and still near the door. The door opens and Bessy rushes in, not seeing Rhiannon, and up to Lord Sarn. She speaks to him with excitement. He relays her tidings. 'More good news. Rebecca is now trying to get into the house by an upper window – and all the military and the police are chasing him somewhere else . . .'

Unnoticed in the general dismay, Rhiannon slips out of the door, leaving Lord Sarn still talking. 'Any gentleman foolish . . .' He only begins the word 'foolish', changing it midway. '. . . willing enough to join in the confusion, follow me!'

He finishes his glass. The male guests make a move towards the door but Lord Sarn's voice halts them. 'Would any gentleman care for some refreshment before he goes? It may be his last chance. No? Then – onwards!'

And, taking a candlestick in his hand, he moves, without hurry towards the door, followed by the male guests. Sir Henry, moving from his corner to join them, turns for a moment to Mr Pugh, who has not moved. 'Aren't *you* going to come?'

Mr Pugh smiles. 'And leave the ladies unprotected?'

Rhiannon's boudoir is very dimly lit. But there is enough light to see that it is a charming and comfortable room in excellent feminine taste, and with a small piano. Rhiannon is standing in front of the looking glass in a corner of the room.

She sees, reflected in the glass, the curtains of the window blowing inwards.

Then the masked figure of Rebecca struggling into the room appears.

She does not turn as Rebecca climbs right into the room. He does not see Rhiannon.

'Close the window! Pull the curtains!'

Rebecca spins round at the sound of her voice, sees her standing in a corner of the room in the dim light. He hesitates, makes a movement as though to climb out of the window again.

'Quickly!'

There is such urgency in her voice that he obeys her, closing the window, pulling the curtains, looking at her the while, as she stands in the dimness some little way from him.

'Take off your disguise. Put it behind these curtains.'

She points to a curtained recess.

She runs to the door, opens it, looks out, hears the noise of men coming up the stairs, closes it again sharply and locks it.

As she does this, Rebecca is rapidly taking off his Rebecca clothes and hiding them in the recess.

She turns from the door, comes down the room towards him. He stands quite still in the shadow of the curtains. She lights a candle on the mantelpiece. And Anthony, in his ordinary dress, steps out of the shadows into the light.

'It's you!'

'I didn't know this was your room.'

Rhiannon is still, hardly able to believe her eyes. 'Anthony!'

Quietly, almost apologetically. 'It was the only window open on the balcony outside.'

'Yes. I opened it for Rebecca.'

'You opened it for *me*!'

The voices of men can be heard in the corridor outside. But neither Anthony nor Rhiannon takes any notice. They stand looking at each other in the middle of the room.

'Oh, Anthony!'

'You are sad because it's me.'

'No.'

'Rebecca should have been a stranger.'

'No, he *couldn't* be a stranger. He *couldn't* have been anyone but you. I know that now.'

'How do you know?'

'Because I *was* in love with you. Although I hated you, sometimes. And I *was* in love with Rebecca, too. And I couldn't love *two* men, could I? Not at the same time. And so you *had* to be Rebecca. You see?'

'Oh, the logic of women!'

The men's voices outside grow nearer and louder. And suddenly there is a banging at the door. And Anthony and Rhiannon are in each other's arms. Lord Sarn can be heard shouting from outside. 'Rhiannon, Rhiannon. Are you safe?'

'Perfectly safe.'

'That fellow Rebecca's in the house.'

Rhiannon smiles at Anthony and says very softly: 'I know. I'm in his arms.'

Lord Sarn's voice calls from beyond the door. 'What did you say? Open the door. He may be hiding in your room.'

'Of course he's not. Don't get so excited, Uncle. You know it makes your nose bleed.' She whispers to Anthony. 'You can't go now. The house'll be surrounded. They'd kill you. No! Stay where you are!'

She kisses him lightly and quickly and runs to the door and opens it, but only partially, to say: 'Come in, Uncle . . . No, nobody else.'

And she lets Lord Sarn come into the room, and closes the door behind him. Lord Sarn complains excitedly: 'I'm *not* excited, my nose isn't bleeding.'

He suddenly sees Anthony, who is sitting on a stool

at the small piano. 'Anthony! What are you doing here? Learning the piano?'

Anthony rises. 'Sir, I must beg your pardon for my presence here.'

'Indeed you must.'

'It is all my fault, Uncle . . .'

'Sir, it is all my fault . . .'

'Don't be so heroic, Anthony. It doesn't suit you.'

'I apologise, sir.'

'Here I am, and every man in the house with me, chasing a desperate criminal – who may even now be hiding behind those curtains . . .' Lord Sarn makes a movement towards the curtains as if to pull them apart and expose Anthony's disguise which is lying there, but Rhiannon intercepts him.

'No, no, Uncle, he isn't, I assure you.'

'And here *you* are in Rhiannon's private sitting-room – though she will call it a boudoir, hiding behind her petticoats.'

'Sir, I . . .'

'Why did you send a letter excusing yourself from the ball tonight? *I* couldn't get out of it; why should *you*?'

Rhiannon takes a hand in the game. 'And why did you sneak upstairs, as you must have done, instead of . . .'

Anthony silences them both, with sudden resolution. 'Sir, I came to ask your ward to be my wife.'

Lord Sarn looks at him in amazement. And Rhiannon's eyes too, are wide, as she looks at Anthony. At this moment, Lord Sarn shouts: 'Lend me your handkerchief – quick!'

Anthony hands him his, and Lord Sarn holds it to his nose, mumbling through it: '*Now* you should be pleased.

My nose *is* bleeding.'

'Oh, Uncle, let me put a key down your back, shall I?'

'Keep away from me. After a night like this, there's no knowing *what* you'd put down my back. Criminals come into my house *disguised* as criminals, dance with my guests, disappear, and are last seen climbing up the ivy like bats. And on top of that, you, you, sir, skulk in when nobody's looking and propose to my ward.' He turns to Rhiannon. 'I hope you said . . .'

She supplies the answer. 'Yes.'

'You *did*?'

'You do?'

Rhiannon and Anthony have eyes only for one another, as Lord Sarn complains, with glum disapproval: 'She does. But that's no excuse for your behaviour. There's a murderer in the house . . .'

'Rebecca hasn't killed anyone!'

'He may have by this time.' In momentary wish-fulfilment – 'Perhaps he's killed Sir Henry. But even if he has, he still must be caught. That's the law.' He moves towards the door. 'Anthony, we'll talk about this again when you're calmer.' He holds the handkerchief more firmly to his bleeding nose. 'Now come with me.'

'Yes, Uncle.'

Anthony opens the door to let Lord Sarn through. Lord Sarn peers up at him with a bewildered frown at the word 'Uncle'. Anthony bows to Rhiannon, and kisses his hand to her, and goes out.

Out on the landing, pandemonium. Up and down the stairs, and in and out of rooms along the corridor, guests, soldiers and police are rushing and impeding each other.

Lord Sarn stands still, looks at the scene in bewilderment. 'It doesn't look at all like home any more.'

Captain Marsden comes up to him. 'Not a sign of him, sir.'

A group of police comes out of a bedroom and march stolidly upstairs. Lord Sarn watches them. 'And it doesn't look as if it will ever be the same again.' He wanders along the corridor, peers in at an open door. Marsden sees Anthony for the first time. He strides up to him. 'Where did *you* come from?'

'I climbed up the ivy.'

'Don't try to make a fool of me. You've been to see Miss Rhiannon.'

Lord Sarn peers out of the open door, calls to Marsden. 'There are soldiers looking under my bed.'

'Yes, sir. On my instructions.'

Marsden turns back to Anthony. 'Keep away from Miss Rhiannon. She knows what you are.'

'That's true. She does.'

'You can't speak out to her like a man. You have to wheedle your way into her room at night and . . .'

Anthony interrupts him. '. . . and now we're quarreling in the corridor. At least, it's a change from the hall.'

Lord Sarn, who has just peered in at his bedroom door, calls out to Marsden. 'There are policemen in the cupboards. Do you suppose they'd like a snooze on my bed?'

Marsden ignores him and says to Anthony: 'Shall we continue our quarrel outside?'

'Not tonight, Captain. I am expected home. Another time.'

'No. Not another time. Now!' He takes Anthony by

the arm and leads him down the stairs. As they near the hall at the foot of the stairs, they hear a confused noise from the morning-room; and, amid the noise, the terrified squeals of women. Marsden runs quickly down the remaining stairs and across the hall to the morning-room. The squeals redouble as he tries to open the morning-room doors. Sir Henry and another guest come running along the hall and try the morning-room door, and hammer at it.

'It's Pugh!' Sir Henry tells Marsden. 'He's alone with the ladies!'

🐚  🐚  🐚

Up in her boudoir, Rhiannon is at the piano, playing softly. Bessy is busy about the room, tidying up and putting away Rhiannon's clothes. She pulls open the curtains that cover the recess and sees Anthony's discarded Rebecca disguise.

'Look what I've found, Miss Rhiannon,' she exclaims. 'They're just like the things Rebecca was wearing, Miss.'

Rhiannon looks round, and suddenly stops playing. 'No. They're quite different, Bessy. They came in a parcel with the other new fancy dresses.'

'But, Miss, these are old clothes. And they *are* just like Rebecca's. Here's the same big black skirt with the same frills and everything. And it's *wet* at the edges, Miss. It's *soaking* wet . . . Just as if somebody's been wearing it in the snow.'

Rhiannon tries to control her agitation. 'Oh, yes, I remember now. I tried it on early this evening.'

'Funny place to try a fancy dress on, Miss – out in the snow. And I was with you all the evening.'

'Yes. You were, weren't you?'

'And it's torn, too, Miss. A horrible big tear. Just as if somebody'd been *climbing* in it. Perhaps when you tried it on in the snow this evening, you climbed up a wall as well.'

'Perhaps I did.'

'Shall I put them away now?'

'Yes, please.'

'I'll put them in the big chest in your bedroom, where nobody'll find them. Where nobody'll know about them except *us*. Perhaps you'll be wanting to try them on again another night. You never know.'

'No. You never know.'

Bessy takes the Rebecca clothes away. Rhiannon starts to play, softly, again. And Bessy comes and begins to comb her hair, with a very little, secret smile on her lips.

It is half an hour later when Anthony enters the front door of Pentre House. He takes off his coat and shakes the snow from it. Sara Jane appears at once, fussily takes his coat, clucks and mothers him. 'There! I knew! Wet through again. Every night the same. You'll catch your death.'

'Why did you stay up for me, Sara Jane? It's late.'

'If I didn't stay up, you'd starve. You can't even boil

a kettle for yourself. Now you go and sit by the fire and I'll bring you a nice . . .'

'Not a nice cup of milk, Sara Jane.'

'With something in it. And a special little pie I baked, but there's only half left now though. I gave the other half to Thomas.'

'How is he, Sara Jane?'

'He's up in the attic on a feather mattress with a hot water jar and the Bible. Cosy as cosy. And religious.'

'You're good, Sara Jane.'

'Oh, and I suppose you don't think you're any good at all. Just risking your life every night for all the people round here and . . .'

'I nearly got caught tonight.'

'Heaven save us!'

'No. Miss Rhiannon saved me.'

'And quite right, too, since you love each other.'

'How did you know?'

'I am a widow, Mister Anthony. The book of love has no closed pages for me.'

'They're sending more troops, Sara Jane.'

'Never you mind. We'll beat them all. Never you grieve or worry, boy bach. What with me and the reverend in the attic, there'll be a lot of praying for Rebecca's Daughters in this house tonight . . .'

Through Pembroke market square march the new troops. Sullen crowds watch them. There is no sound save for the marching feet of the soldiers on the cobbles and the barked out commands. The crowds remain still and silent. Even the children, who normally at the sight of soldiers would shout and play and mock-march with them, are silent as their elders. In the front fringe of the crowd, Bessy and Sara Jane are standing together. And most of the soldiers passing by have an eye for Bessy at her plump prettiest. One strapping soldier, at the end of the line nearest Bessy, gives her a slow, deliberate and very meaning wink. And Bessy is raising her little mittened hand discreetly and secretly to wave at him when down comes Sara Jane's hand on hers, with a sharp smack which rings out in the silence of the crowd.

Standing close together in the crowd, Rhodri Huws, Shoni Fawr and old William Evan speak softly among themselves. 'Look at 'em! Men just like us – and they come to shoot us down!'

'A shame the hens aren't laying. I could use their eggs.'

'Men like us who never had anything and never will have. Who'll die as poor as they were born. What do they want with Turnpike Trusts? What'll the creepin' lords and squires do for them? They should be fighting with us.'

'We don't want no fighting,' William Evan tells him.

'Talk for yourself, you old bird of peace.'

'Fighting won't get us nowhere.'

'Ach, you old dove!'

'You got to trust Sir John Watkyn,' maintains William, stubbornly.

'You got to trust Rebecca!'

'Leave Sir John to have a go at the Prime Minister. You wait! He'll get him to listen.'

'Prime Ministers don't listen. Prime Ministers don't care about us.'

'Who *do* they care about then?'

'Prime Ministers.'

In a room at No. 10, Downing Street, Sir John Watkyn is having an audience of the Prime Minister and the Home Secretary. The Prime Minister shakes his head and tells him: 'I still fail to understand how I can be expected to condone the behaviour of your wild Welsh friends, Sir John. You speak eloquently for them. You would have me see them as martyrs and champions of liberty. I cannot see them in that light. On the evidence you have brought before me, they are wilfully misguided persons guilty of wanton and widespread destruction of property . . .'

'Sir, I am not attempting to make you condone their acts, but to sympathise with their reasons. And God knows, sir, they have reasons enough.'

'They should express their disapproval of existing legislature through the proper channels,' says the Home Secretary.

'But, sir, the proper channels are stuffed and choked with prejudice. It is the men in authority themselves who derive profits from the preposterous charges levied at the tollgates. All I ask now is that a Royal Commission be set up to investigate the whole system. And I warrant that the result will be . . .'

The Prime Minister cuts him short: 'You are hardly

in such an omniscient position, Sir John, as to warrant beforehand what the findings of a Royal Commission will be – even if I were to authorise the setting up of one. And it is plain that the idea of a Commission can not be countenanced while these – what do they call themselves, these wild Welshman of yours?'

'Rebecca's Daughters, sir.'

'Ah, yes. A very Biblical people, the Welsh. While Rebecca's Daughters continue their activities.'

'No, sir. But if I can go back to them and tell them that there is to be a Commission, then I am sure that not another gate will be attacked. They only want justice . . .'

'Such a small thing to want in this world!'

'And that is why I came to you, sir. Let me go back and tell them *now*, before there is any bloodshed, before there are any open clashes with the troops. Let us prevent that, sir. These are passionate and honest men.'

'I admire their honesty, but deplore their passion. If you can guarantee that they keep it within bounds – and stop all this swashbuckling nonsense – we really cannot have hordes of masked men disguised as old women howling up and down the country roads all night – then I think your appeal to our sense of justice will not have been in vain.'

'I *will* guarantee it, sir,' says Sir John, exultantly. 'Let me tell them the great news, and there will not be another single act of destruction. Rebecca's Daughters will not meet again.'

A figure moves cautiously along under shelter of houses, stopping here and there to thrust something under a door or through an open window. In the shadows on the other side of the street, another figure watches. The first figure goes down the dark street and is lost. And the second figure stealthily crosses the street and withdraws a piece of paper from under a door. He unfolds and reads it. He is Idris Evans the blacksmith.

🦢    🦢    🦢

Lord Sarn, standing before the cheval mirror in his bedroom, is dressing for dinner. His valet, Beynon, a prim and self-righteous person, is tying his tie for him.

'I wish,' says Lord Sarn, 'I had a tie you could pull out like this and let it go smack during dinner. Especially if the rector is dining.'

'Very amusing, my lord.'

Lord Sarn looks at Beynon who wears a look of cold, unsmiling, aloof disapproval. 'We must have a good laugh about it one day together.'

'Yes, my lord.'

The tie tied, Beynon helps Lord Sarn into his coat. 'My lord, there have been rumours in the kitchen.'

'I am sure there have. It is an excellent place for them. They help the cooking. Rumour and pepper, a pinch of both, and there you are.'

'Very alarming rumours, my lord.'

'Not that little parlour-maid – again?'

'No, my lord. More alarming.'

'Somebody has stolen the Napoleon brandy? Dave Button is leaving? The cook is a poisoner?'

'No, my lord, but it *is* about David Button. It is rumoured below stairs,' Beynon's voice sinks, 'that he is one of Rebecca's Daughters!'

'Impossible! I knew his father well.'

'I had it from my usually impeccable sources of information, my lord.'

'*Quite* impossible. He is the best coachman in the country. I trust no-one else to drive me. He never rattles and he never goggles.'

'The constable who was guarding Mr Mordecai Thomas in the lock-up told me in confidence, my lord, that he thought he recognised the voice of David Button when he was attacked that night, my lord.'

'I cannot believe it. Nobody so considerate of his passengers could possibly attack a constable. Now if it had been the coachman who was here *before* Dave Button – I would put nothing past him. He drove like a fiend. One part of me was permanently black and blue.'

'You wouldn't consider, my lord, confronting him with the charge?'

'Certainly not. If he is what you say, then – er – we'll keep a close eye on him. We may learn something that way.'

Beynon does not attempt to hide his disapproval. 'Very good, my lord.'

'Now, who did you say was waiting for me downstairs?'

'Captain Marsden, and the police officer, and the blacksmith.'

'Perhaps they want me to make a fourth at whist.

Tell them I'll be down at once.'

As Beynon bows and withdraws, Lord Sarn looks at himself in the mirror and says to his reflection. 'Dismiss our Dave! Not if he were Rebecca himself!' A doubt comes into his mind. 'Perhaps he is!'

When Lord Sarn comes down, he finds the police inspector and Captain Marsden waiting in the morning-room. Sheepishly and foxily, Idris Evans, the blacksmith, stands a little way from them.

'What is it now?' says his lordship peremptorily. 'My dinner's panting on the table. Found Rebecca?'

He asks the last question a little shiftily, not looking at Marsden or the police inspector in the eye.

'Not yet, my lord.'

Lord Sarn breathes his relief and sits at the table. The inspector hands him a slip of paper. 'But we found a message from him. Pushed under a doorway.'

'*I* picked it up, your lordship,' says Idris Evans, ingratiatingly.

Lord Sarn appears to notice him for the first time. He looks at him with dislike; then turns to the inspector and Marsden.

'The informer?'

'Yes, sir.'

Lord Sarn looks back at Idris. 'Stay shoeing horses, my man. An honourable trade. Keep to your anvil, or one day you'll be shod.'

And Idris Evans looks down.

Lord Sarn glances at the paper and frowns as he reads it. 'Queer message. "My love is like a red, red rose" very complimentary.' He looks up at Idris Evans. 'You say you found it?'

'Yes, your lordship.'

'It obviously doesn't apply to *you* . . . Except that Judas was supposed to wear red. "My love is like a red, red rose . . .".'

Idris Evans breaks in: 'Rhos Goch! There is a place called Rhos Goch!'

'And the English call it Red Roses.' Lord Sarn looks up at the inspector. 'That sounds what you want.'

Marsden pulls out a map from his pocket, spreads it on the table. 'Here, sir! See, here's the place.'

Lord Sarn and the police Inspector bend over the map and Marsden says: 'Now for my plan. This place is in section four. Tonight . . .'

'You're certain it *will* be tonight?'

'Yes, sir. Tonight, we put up four lanterns on the guard house here. These will act as a signal to the troops on the other side of the estuary. They will know where to – concentrate!'

And the Inspector adds, happily: 'There'll be some dead Daughters tonight!'

Mrs Dave Button, a comfortable body, sits comfortably in front of the kitchen fire, darning a pair of man's socks. Bessy hurries in, looking frightened and gasps: 'Oh, Mrs Button!'

Mrs Button does not look up, but imitates Bessy's tone of voice: 'Oh, Bessy Williams!'

'I got to tell someone, Mrs Button . . .'

And Mrs Button looks up at her, sternly. 'You've been listening again to what you oughtn't. I can always tell. The tips of your ears go pink – and quite right, too!'

'I been meaning to tell you ever since I heard but I was frightened.'

'And you *should* be frightened, too. It's a very wicked habit. When Miss Rhiannon listens to what she oughtn't, that's quite different. She wants to know what's going on. But with you, it's just curiosity and curiosity killed the cat.'

'Oh, but it's killing I heard about, Mrs Button, ma'am. Rebecca's Daughters are out tonight and the Captain knows and his lordship and the peeler and everybody. Idris Evans, blacksmith, told them. "There'll be some dead Daughters tonight", they said . . .'

Mrs Button, with surprising agility for her weight, dashes out of the room.

In his bedroom, Dave Button is getting ready for the raid. A woman's black dress lies out on the bed. There is a lighted candle on the dressing table. Dave, a burnt cork in his hand and his face half-blackened, turns quickly as he hears the sound of a door opening. Mrs Button enters, breathlessly: 'Oh, Dave! Dave! . . .'

'What is it, love, don't you like your Sambo?'

'You can't go tonight, Dave. Bessy heard them talking. They know where you're going and . . . Don't go with them tonight, Dave, don't! They'll *kill* you all.'

But Dave Button is up and out of the room, leaving Mrs Button tearfully appealing to nothing.

🐑     🐑     🐑

Up in her bedroom, Rhiannon turns as Bessy comes hurrying in. 'Why didn't you come before, Bessy? I've been ringing the bell like a muffin man. And what's the matter with you?'

'There's nothing the matter, miss.'

'Your hands are trembling. Just like Sir Henry's after a visit to London with his cat. You'd better go to bed. And Bessy . . .'

'Yes, miss?' She looks at her terrified, on the brink of tears.

'Now do stop looking at me like that. Nobody's going to kill you.'

'Oh, Miss Rhiannon.'

'I want you to tell Dave Button – tell him very quietly, don't let anyone else hear – to bring the carriage round to the back of the house, the *back* you understand? I want him to drive me over to Mr Anthony's. And I don't want anyone else to know.'

'He can't, miss.'

'Why can't he?'

'He's gone.'

'Gone where? What's wrong tonight? Have you been having an at-home in the kitchen?'

'He's gone out.'

'Of course he's gone *out,* if he's gone at all. Oh,

Bessy, don't stand there sniffling and sobbing. If you want to burst into tears, here's my handkerchief.' She hands her handkerchief to Bessy who cries into it. 'But you must tell me *why* you're crying.'

'I can't . . .'

'You *must*. How can I help you if you don't. We're friends, aren't we, Bessy? We haven't got many secrets from each other . . . I think you know *my* secret, don't you, even though we've never talked to each other about it . . .'

'He's gone to Rebecca, miss . . . They're going to catch Rebecca's Daughters tonight and . . .'

Now the two girls are very close together, Rhiannon holding Bessy's hands.

'Tell me everything. Quickly, Bessy. I must go to Rebecca, too. *Tell* me, Bessy!'

◎      ◎      ◎

Rhiannon rides hard up the drive of Pentre House, dismounts in front of the house, runs up the steps, beats on the door. The door is opened by Sara Jane. Rhiannon, carrying a dark bundle of clothing over her arm, asks: 'Where's Mister Anthony?'

'Couldn't tell to be sure, miss. He's not in the house, that I do know.'

'Let me in, Sara Jane.'

'Now, it's late for you to be out, Miss Rhiannon. His lordship will be anxious . . .'

Rhiannon pushes her way past Sara Jane into the hall. And there, behind the open door, is Dave Button.

126

'Where has he gone?' she asks.

'Who, Miss Rhiannon?'

'Mister Anthony . . . Rebecca!'

Dave Button and Sara Jane exchange startled glances.

'Oh, can't you see? I'm one of you,' says Rhiannon impatiently. 'Look at *these,* if you don't believe me . . .' She slings down a bundle of clothing on to a chair. 'They're *his* clothes, Rebecca's clothes . . . Where is he, Sara Jane! I love him.'

'He's gone. Alone.'

'He wouldn't let me go with him,' confirms Dave. 'He's gone to the guard house to smash the signal lantern.'

And Sara Jane adds in a flat, grief-stricken voice: 'He said he didn't have time to disguise himself. And he went unarmed. He always said there must be shooting and killing. And now it's him that'll be killed.

⚉　　⚉　　⚉

High up on the guard house, four points of light shine clearly and brightly. Beyond them the estuary is dark.

Two soldiers come out of the darkness. One points towards the guard house. The other raises a lantern above his head, swings it four times as a signal.

Around the opposite side of the guard house, Anthony is slowly clambering up on to the roof. A glow from above indicates that he is nearing the lanterns.

In the roadway, a soldier is leaning on his carbine, watching the lights. The tune he has been whistling suddenly stops. One of the lights is obscured. The soldier stiffens into action and raises his carbine.

Anthony has climbed up on to a level with one of the lanterns. He stretches out a hand to grasp it. The sound of a shot. He falls out of picture.

Now, Anthony is lying face downwards on the ground. He squirms over and raises himself. He feels his shoulder and side. His hand comes away dripping with blood. Painfully, awkwardly, he gets to his feet and starts off into the darkness at a shambling run. Two more shots are heard. He flings himself to the ground, then, after a moment, staggers to his feet again and lurches off. Near him now is the sound of the estuary water.

Two soldiers run out of darkness. One lowers his lantern and says 'Follow the blood!' And they run into the darkness.

Anthony lurches on to the bank of the estuary. A shot whines over his head. He falls on to the bank and rolls over into the darkness. A moment later, the two soldiers appear. One lowers his lantern again and says: 'The blood's stopped.'

'My last shot got him,' claims the other. They peer out through the darkness. There is nothing to be seen but the dark water. Their voices are strangely clear across the night water.

'He's feeding the fish. What's the kind of fish in these waters, Albert?'

'Welsh fish. And now they got a Daughter . . .'

They move away. Anthony creeps out of the darkness and silently into the water. He swims on one side, his other arm dangling uselessly behind him like a long weed on the water.

Minutes later, he comes out of the darkness, soaking wet and wounded, and makes his way painfully, at the end of his tether, to the back door of Pentre House. Slowly, he manages to lift the catch of the door and open it.

Rhiannon, Dave Button and Sara Jane are standing near the kitchen fire. Suddenly, at the sound of the opening door, they turn around and Rhiannon cries: 'Anthony!'

He leans heavily against the door, water dripping from him, blood staining and patching his side and shoulder. With an attempt at lightness, he smiles and says: 'Good evening, my dear.'

Now Rhiannon, Dave Button and Sara Jane rush up to him and support him and lead him gently to a chair where they sit him down.

'Get his coat off! He's wounded,' orders Rhiannon.

Anthony smiles. 'The Welsh fish bit me.'

They tear his coat off. The clothing beneath is blood-soaked. Rhiannon turns to Dave Button. 'Dave, ride and fetch the doctor. Nothing matters now.'

Dave makes a move as if to go, but Anthony's voice, though harsh with pain, is strong enough to stop him. 'You go, Dave, and I'll rise from the dead and haunt you. *Everything* matters now. I didn't change the lights. I failed. But *you* mustn't. Maybe there's still time. There *must* be time. You and everyone else you can trust, ride and warn them. Warn then *now*. Ride till your horse drops. Never mind if they're with us or not. Warn them all. *They must not raid Rhos Goch.*'

'Yes, Mister Anthony . . .'

'I'm Rebecca, dead or alive – d'you hear, my darling Daughter? *Leave Rhos Goch alone.* Attack the Carew gate.'

His head slumps forward on his bloody arm, and

Sara Jane takes control. '*I'll* look after him. *I'll* fetch the doctor for him if I got to ride a donkey there. Follow your instructions, Dave Button. And, Miss Rhiannon, you help me . . .'

She turns to where Rhiannon was standing. But Rhiannon is not there. A second later, she runs into the kitchen with the Rebecca clothes in her arms. Sara Jane stares at her aghast. 'What are you doing?'

'Help me get into these. *Please, Sara Jane . . .*'

<br>

Rhiannon, dressed as Rebecca, and Dave Button, galloping through darkness up to a division of the road. A high wind tossing the black roadside trees. At the division, Dave Button rides one way, Rhiannon the other.

Rhiannon riding through darkness into a farmyard. She pulls up under the farmhouse window, cups her hands, and calls. We cannot hear her voice for the music and the noise of the high wind. The window opens and a man's head appears. Under his thatch of light hair, the man's face is black as coal. Rhiannon, calling her instructions through wind and music, points, her arm outstretched, through the darkness away to the left. The man at the window nods vigorously and closes the window as Rhiannon turns and rides off.

Dave Button riding up to a row of small cottages. Quickly he dismounts, runs to the first cottage, hammers on the door. The door is opened by a man already half-disguised as a Rebecca-ite. We see Dave speak to him urgently, but do not hear his voice for wind and music. Dave mounts again and rides off, and the Rebecca-ite hurries to the next cottage and hammers on the door.

Rhiannon riding out of darkness into another farm-yard. A lantern is shining in an outhouse. She rides up to the outhouse and calls. Through the open outhouse door comes a group of three farm labourers, shotguns slung over their shoulders. Again, Rhiannon speaks and beckons her instructions and the men, as she turns and rides off, run across the yard to where their waiting horses are tethered.

Soldiers in rowboats crossing the dark estuary waters towards the four-pointed signal at the top of Rhos Goch guard house.

Rhiannon and Dave Button riding over a dark field towards a wood. Out of the wood comes a group of mounted Rebecca-ites. Rhiannon holds up her hand, and the horse-men stop. Rhiannon, speaking through wind and music, gestures the horsemen to another direction from that which they were taking, and the horsemen, saluting Rhiannon-as-Rebecca, ride off that way.

Soldiers grounding their rowboats on the estuary shore beneath Rhos Goch guard house and scrambling out and up towards the four-pointed signal.

Dave Button and Rhiannon riding on to the top of the quarry. Below them is a group of Rebecca-ites standing by their horses. Rhiannon calls down to them, and signals them to follow her. And the Rebecca-ites jump on their horses and ride towards her. Rhiannon and Dave Button turn and are off.

Rhiannon and Dave Button riding into a valley farm and shouting their instructions to a small group of Rebecca-ites in the yard preparing for the road, muffling their horses' hooves, strapping on saws and pick-axes to their saddles.

Rhiannon and Dave Button at the head of a company of mounted Rebecca-ites riding through darkness towards the Carew tollgate.

At the Rhos Goch tollgate, the soldiers are preparing to meet Rebecca's raid. Under the superintendence of Captain Marsden they conceal themselves in a deep ditch outside of the tollgate, lie down in the ditch with their carbines levelled over the top. Captain Marsden directs other soldiers into the tollgate-house itself, there to wait in concealment at the windows.

Marsden speaks quietly to one of his officers: 'Rebecca – dead or alive. Those are my instructions. But you can forget that last word.'

'I've been thinking, sir – what if Rebecca was Lord Sarn himself.'

'Then we should be saved the trouble of shooting. He's been dead for years.'

Suddenly the officer points excitedly into the dark distance. 'Look, sir!'

In the distance, the bright glow of some great fire is burning the dark sky.

'It's the Carew Gate!' shouts the inspector.

They look at the fire, growing every moment brighter, in silence for a moment. Then Marsden, with barely controlled rage, says 'I wish I had joined the navy. They have a larger vocabulary. You can call the men off.'

And he turns and moves back towards the tollgate.

The soldiers come out of concealment, grumbling among themselves. They sling their carbines back over their shoulders.

'They're not playing fair . . .'

'Think I'll join Rebecca . . .'

Grumbling, they sit down at the road edge.

'Only shot a rabbit since I been here . . .'

'And that was tough as a boot . . .'

'One rabbit, and a nasty black crow.'

Grumbling, the soldiers lean against the tollhouse, their rifles against the wall, squat on the road edge, wander about disconsolately.

Suddenly out of the pitch darkness two horses, mounted by Rhiannon and Dave Button, gallop furiously past them, jettisoning a big bundle nearly at Marsden's feet. Then the horsemen are gone, galloping in a flash past the soldiers, caught unawares as they squat or loiter on the roadside. Too late the soldiers retrieve their carbines and fire after the vanished horses.

Marsden and the police inspector bend over the big bundle. It is Idris Evans the blacksmith, trussed and gagged. Pinned to his Rebecca-ite clothing is a note which reads: ONE INFORMER RETURNED WITHOUT THANKS – REBECCA.

Marsden leaves the trussed body and runs towards the tollhouse, where several horses are tethered. Marsden jumps on to one. Rapidly, his officers mount the others. They all gallop off into the darkness after Rhiannon and Dave Button.

Rhiannon-as-Rebecca and Dave Button gallop up the driveway and around the side of the house, near the paddock. They dismount. Working fast and expertly, they unsaddle the horses.

'Hide the saddles in the loft,' Rhiannon tells Dave. 'Then get to bed. *Quickly*.'

'Yes, Miss – Rebecca,' says Dave and runs off into the darkness with the saddles.

Rhiannon opens the paddock gates, and lets the horses loose. Rapidly, she removes her Rebecca clothing, makes a big ball of it, and wedges it into the dense shrubbery around the paddock. Then she runs towards the back kitchen door of the house.

Up the driveway ride Captain Marsden and his officers. They jump off their horses. They run up the steps. Marsden hammers on the door. There is deadly silence in the house. He hammers again.

Lord Sarn's manservant, in his night-shirt, carrying a candle in one hand and an ancient blunderbuss in the other, comes timidly downstairs, glancing apprehensively at the shadows cast by the candles. Deadly stillness in the house. Then the hammering crashes into the silence again, and the manservant nearly drops his candle and blunderbuss. He hurries on downstairs into the hall.

Outside, Captain Marsden hammering on the door, his officers on the steps behind him. Presently it is opened by the manservant. He has his blunderbuss raised to his shoulder. His candle stands on a table in the hall just behind him. Marsden pushes the blunderbuss aside. 'Let me in! And put that thing back in the Ark.'

Lowering his blunderbuss, the manservant moves aside to allow Marsden and his men to enter. As they do so, Marsden says: 'Take me to his lordship's bedroom.'

'He won't like that, sir.'

'Lead the way!'

The manservant reluctantly takes up the candle and leads the way. Marsden and the officers follow him along the hall and up the stairs.

'He's terrible hard to wake, sir,' grumbles the manservant. 'And when he wakes he's terrible. He throws things, sir. He threw the clock at me once. I had to have three stitches.'

They go on up the stairs and along the corridor. The manservant stops before a door and reluctantly knocks; a little timid tap.

'Louder!' orders Marsden.

The manservant taps again, only just a little louder.

'LOUDER!'

And Marsden himself pounds on the door. The manservant looks terrified. 'It won't be three stitches after this. I'll be in a bath-chair.' From within comes a loud and angry cry. 'That's him! Like a lion's den!'

'Go in!'

'I'm no Samuel.'

'Tell him I must see him. At once.'

He opens the door, pushes the cowering manservant in, closes it behind him. There is a loud and angry cry from Lord Sarn, a pathetic bleat from the manservant, and a crash of crockery. Grimly, Marsden waits. Slowly the door opens, the manservant appears. He is holding his hand to his eye and speaks shakily. 'He'll see you now.'

Marsden goes into the bedroom alone, leaving his officers outside. One of them asks the manservant: 'What did he throw at you?'

'That's right.'

Lord Sarn, nightcapped, sitting wrathfully up in bed,

surveys Marsden. 'Mad drunk servants armed with blunder-busses breaking the door down and throwing the china about. Profligate soldiery lurching in with their great muddy-blood-stained boots! This is not a pot-house, sir. This is the private bedroom of one small, harmless peer! What do you want?'

'Sir, I must –'

'The answer is No! Go away! Go to bed!'

'Sir, I must search the house.'

Lord Sarn looks at the ceiling. 'Land of my fathers, give me strength! This English baboon must now search my house in the middle of the night . . . What for, Captain Ape?'

'Rebecca, my lord.'

'Rebecca again! Why doesn't the fellow move in as a lodger? Go on, search the house then! Comb the cupboards, delve in the drawers. You'll probably find some old police-men left over from your last visit . . .'

Marsden turns to go, and Lord Sarn gropes his way across to a side-table on which stands a tray with a bottle and a glass.

On the landing, the officers and the manservant are standing waiting for Marsden. When he appears, he says: 'We'll search every room.' And leads the way to the next door to Lord Sarn's demanding: 'Who sleeps here?'

'Nobody,' says the manservant.

Marsden opens the door. 'We'll see if he's in bed.'

One of the officers goes into the room, returns a moment later and shakes his head. 'Nobody.'

'That's what I said.'

Marsden moves to the next room. 'Who's in there?'

'Same person.'

The officer again goes in to search, again returns and shakes his head.

Up to the floor above. As Marsden opens another door, the manservant protests: 'Not that one, sir. That's . . .'

Marsden waves his men on into the room. Inside, there is a sudden little squeal and then a giggle. The manservant looks at Marsden reprovingly. 'That's Bessy's room.'

There is a long moment's silence; then another little muffled giggle. Marsden calls sharply: 'Come out!'

And the officers come out rather sheepishly. Marsden glares at them and then moves down the landing. He stops at the furthest door.

'That's where Dave Button's *supposed* to sleep,' says the manservant, slyly. 'If you ask me, *he* won't be there . . .'

Marsden gestures to his men to enter the room. From within comes the sound of resonant snoring. The manservant looks astonished. 'Well, if he *is* there, he's been drinking.'

The officers come out of the room. 'Dead asleep, sir,' reports one.

☺   ☺   ☺

Now the search is in the other wing and they are outside Rhiannon's boudoir. From within comes the sound of the piano. Marsden knocks; the music stops and Rhiannon's voice says: 'Come in, please.'

Marsden opens the door. Rhiannon is seated at the piano, dressed in a pegnoir.

'I beg your pardon, Miss Rhiannon,' says Marsden gruffly.

Rhiannon looks at him coolly. 'But why? This is quite a correct social hour to call – three o'clock in the morning.'

'Do you always play the piano at three in the morning?'

'No, sometimes I play the flute.' Then the tone of her voice changes to an icy anger. 'What concern is it of yours what I do or when?'

'None. None, of course, but Rebecca . . .'

'Is *not* in my room. I do not allow men in my room at night. I said "men", Captain Marsden. That obviously does not include you. Good night.'

And she plays, very softly, the little 'Rebecca' tune – 'It was in the year eighteen forty three,' as, with a curt bow, Marsden goes out.

🐦  🐦  🐦

Lord Sarn, sitting up in bed, is drinking port, as Marsden returns. He looks at him reproachfully and says: 'You woke me up when I was dreaming about mermaids . . .'

'I am sorry, my lord.'

'Why should *you* be sorry I dream about mermaids? And you ransack the house and find – nothing. I'll have the law on you, Captain Marsden. If it comes to that, I *am* the law. Good!' He rubs his hands together in anticipation of a pleasant dressing-down when the door opens and one of the officers rushes in. 'Don't knock,' says Lord Sarn politely. 'Come right in!'

'We found two horses in the paddock, sir,' reports

the officer. 'Just unsaddled, too, by the looks of them.'

Marsden looks at Lord Sarn. 'Whose horses could *they* be, sir?'

'After tonight I wouldn't be surprised if they were old Nick's and his mother's.' In a temper. 'How do I know? Ask Dave Button!' Then a sudden look of alarm crosses his face as he repeats 'Dave Button! No, no, don't ask Dave Button!'

'He's asleep in his room, sir.'

'Really? Splendid! I wonder what he's dreaming about. Perhaps he's got my mermaids. Good luck to him!' And so relieved is he that he swallows a whole tumbler of port at a gulp and nearly dies of a choking fit.

☙      ☙      ☙

At Anthony's bedside, next morning, Rhiannon and Sara Jane listen as Doctor Rowlands tells his patient: 'A very narrow escape, Mr Raine. Another few inches to the left, and I would have lost a patient, Miss Rhiannon would have lost a husband . . .'

'. . . and Sara Jane wouldn't have anyone to bully into drinking bread-and-milk.'

'These poachers of yours must be very desperate fellows. They don't often shoot at squires, you know. Perhaps it's because they're uneatable. Did you see their faces?'

'No.'

'Maybe they were masked like Rebecca's Daughters,' suggests the doctor, and looks from face to face, his eyebrows lifted quizzically. In his manner, not his words, he makes it plain that he knows the story of the poachers is untrue and guesses who Anthony really is. 'Another few inches to the left, and, who knows, Rebecca's Daughters may have lost their . . .'

'Yes, doctor?' prompts Rhiannon quickly.

'. . . why, one of their bitterest enemies, of course.'

'Of course,' confirms Anthony. 'But I doubt if Rebecca can keep fighting much longer.'

'Oh, Mr Anthony!' from Sara Jane.

Anthony smiles up at her. 'That would be a *good* thing, wouldn't it, Sara Jane? No, there's too much against him. Sooner or later, it's bound to come to an open fight. I don't want bloodshed here.'

'Perhaps there has been some blood shed already,' suggests the doctor.

'What does one man matter? It's all those others — they mustn't be massacred. No, doctor. Rebecca can't go on. Injustice wins in the end.'

The doctor gets up from the bedside and puts his medical equipment into his bag. As he does so, he speaks, quite casually, without looking at any of his listeners. 'I came through the town this morning. There were notices everywhere. A Royal Commission has been appointed to enquire into the – *your* word, Mr Raine – the *injustices* of the Tollgate System. Very interesting reading.'

'Very!'

Dr Rowlands has packed his bag and is moving towards the door. At the door, he turns. 'There is only one condition – Rebecca's Daughters must cease their activities. These are the official words, you understand; personally, I would say they must stop their nonsense before anyone *else* gets hurt. They must cease their activities while the Commision is sitting. I hope Rebecca takes the news to heart.'

'He will.'

'Perhaps he has, already. Good-day, Mr Raine.'

'Good-day – and thank you, Doctor.'

An influential group is meeting in the morning-room of Sarn Hall. There is Lord Sarn and Captain Marsden, Sir Henry Price-Parry, and Sir John Watkyn.

'If only we knew who Rebecca was!' says Sir John. And Sir Henry tells him: 'I thought *you* were Rebecca once, me boy. Changed me mind after the beggar trussed me up like a chicken. I knew you wouldn't do that!'

'Wouldn't he?' asks Lord Sarn. 'Why not?'

Sir John returns to his serious note. 'If only we did know, we could appeal to him personally, tell him that no proceedings would be taken against him – so long as he stopped his raids.'

But Lord Sarn refuses to be serious. '*I'd* truss you up like a chicken. Any day,' he tells Sir Henry affably. And that worthy replies, with dignity: 'Sarn, you overstep yourself. If it were not for your advanced age . . .'

'*My* age! You rocked me in my cradle. And very unsteady you were. It has probably unbalanced me all my life.' He turns to Sir John. 'You think that if we were to appeal to Rebecca himself, he'd agree to put an end to all this?'

'I do, my lord.'

'Then, with great reluctance, I *may* be able to help you.' He rises, crosses to the bell-pull, pulls it, and returns to his seat. 'It's very sad. He drove like an angel. I'll have to engage another driver and then, oh, my poor springs.'

'You mean you know who he is?' growls Sir Henry. 'I'll pepper the blackguard!'

Lord Sarn's manservant enters. Very sadly his master says: 'Tell Dave Button to come in. Tell him to come slowly . . . Will you join me in a sad drink, gentlemen?' He pours drinks into the glasses on the table. There is a knock on the door. 'Come in, our Dave!'

Dave Button comes in and stands before the collected company at the table. Lord Sarn addresses him. 'David Jonathan Button . . .'

Dave looks at his master in alarm at the unwonted gravity of his voice and the formal use of his name.

'I have, I am afraid, something very serious to ask you. I have known you now for some years, and never has there been a more faithful and skilful coachman – even after elderberry wine. David Jonathan Button, are you or are you not . . .'

His voice is drowned in the noise of galloping hooves from outside. There is a sudden crash of broken glass and a stone flies through the window, landing on the carpet near Lord Sarn's feet. The noise of the galloping hooves grows less, fades into the distance and is gone. Lord Sarn bends down to pick up the stone. 'More high jinks!' Tied to it is a piece of paper. Lord Sarn reads from it, aloud: 'From this moment, Rebecca's Daughters will stop their attacks upon the tollgates so that the Royal Commission can carry out its duties. Signed Rebecca.'

Captain Marsden, who rushed out of the room when

the stone entered it, now returns to say: 'He's gone.'

'Yes,' observes Lord Sarn dryly, 'I thought we heard him go. Well, Sir John?'

'There is nothing else, sir.' He rises. David Button coughs. 'You were asking me a question, my lord. Was I, or was I not . . . ?'

Lord Sarn turns his attention to Dave. He smiles. 'I had forgotten . . . David Jonathan Button, are you or are you not satisfied with your position in this house?'

'I am, my lord, indeed I am!'

'Then from this moment on, there will be an augmentation of your emolument . . .'

Dave Button is near prostrated with grief. 'Oh, your lordship!'

'He means you get more money, you fool,' growls Sir Henry.

'*Thank you,* your lordship. And good health to you!'

Lord Sarn raises his glass. 'Good health to us all!'

The others – even Marsden – echo his sentiments and, from under the table, where he is lapping wine from a saucer, comes the voice of Sir Henry's cat, saying: 'Miaow!'

◈   ◈   ◈

The gentlemen are still drinking. Suddenly, an under-gardener rushes in in a state of excitement. He carries a bundle of clothing. 'Lord Sarn, Lord Sarn, sir!'

'You interrupt our celebrations.'

'I found these in the paddock shrubbery, my lord.'

He puts the clothes down on the table. Lord Sarn

143

backs away from them with distaste. Captain Marsden picks them up hastily, unfolds them. One by one, he holds up in front of the company the various items of Rebecca's clothing. 'Rebecca's skirt . . . Rebecca's blouse . . . Rebecca's petticoat . . . Rebecca's . . .'

Lord Sarn looks at the faces of his guests, stares hard at Marsden, then turns to the under-gardener, interrupting Marsden. 'Take them away and burn them!'

Marsden protests. 'But, my lord, they're evidence! They'll prove that . . .'

Lord Sarn's voice is stern and authoritative. 'I am master of this house. *Burn them*!' And the under-gardener takes Rebecca's clothes from the hands of the amazed Captain Marsden.

☙   ☙   ☙

On to a roaring fire are thrown, one by one, the garments of Rebecca's disguise. The flames snatch and devour them.

On to another, greater fire are thrown the sawn and dismembered pieces of a tollgate. Drawing back from the fire, we see the work of destruction is being carried out under the official direction of Sir John Watkyn, the police, and the troops. The flames rise higher.

For a moment, they light up the faces of Anthony and Rhiannon, smiling and close together.